MW00570981

MYSTERIOUS ONTARIO

Myths, Murders, Mysteries and Legends

Geordie Tefler

QUAGMIRE PRESS

The Publisher: Quagmire Press Ltd.
Website: www.quagmirepress.com

Library and Archives Canada Cataloguing in Publication

Telfer, Geordie
    Mysterious Ontario / Geordie Telfer.

Includes bibliographical references.
ISBN 978-1-926695-17-4

    1. Parapsychology—Ontario. 2. Supernatural. 3. Curiosities and won-ders—Ontario. I. Title.

BF1028.5.C3T45 2012   130.9713   C2012-901317-X

Project Director: Hank Boer
Project Editor: Nicholle Carrière
Cover Image: © Sandralise | Dreamstime.com
Image credits: Every effort has been made to accurately credit the sources of photographs and illustrations. Any errors or omissions should be reported directly to the publisher for correction in future editions. Images courtesy of *The Hamilton Spectator* (pp. 165, 166); Robin Mader (p. 183); *Newark Daily Advocate* (p. 242); Geordie Telfer (pp. 9, 10, 14, 18, 19, 48, 54, 58, 61, 62, 71, 77, 112, 198, 231); *The Toronto Star* (p. 191).

Produced with the assistance of the Government of Alberta, **Government**
Alberta Multimedia Development Fund   **of Alberta** ■

PC: 1

Dedication

~

For Valin—a mystery, a wonder and a miracle all rolled into one

Contents

Acknowledgements

~

All my thanks to Rose and Keith Telfer (my parents), Kim Moore, Robin Mader, Jeff Telfer, Chris Telfer, Neal Bridgens, Barb Leith, Liako Dertilis, Danielle Holke, Collin Douma, Finnegan, Diane and Shawn Murenbeeld, Ava, Tricia Griffith, Michael MacGregor, Deb and Chris Hession, Cooper, Cole, Georgina Lopez, Evan Williams, Indiana, George and Vanessa Laramee, Larissa, Silas, Rob Pazdro, Joanne Foot, Mike Sopora, Cecil, TC, Gus, Chris Quirk, Tiffany Lyndall Knight, John James Hong, Oscar, Lucy, Colleen Zimmerman, Ryan Lippert, Kirsten Hurd, Imogen, Evelyn, Rebecca Quigley, Chris Macbride, Hersh and Ally Jacob, Nicholle Carrière, Dr. David Gotlib, Joanne MacIver, University of Toronto Libraries, Toronto Central Reference Library and last but not least, the many helpful archivists at the Archives of Ontario.

Introduction

~

Mystery is possibility. What could the answer possibly be? How could the solution change our lives? Is it possible that there are some mysteries whose answers are better left unknown? Even though we spend a lot of time and effort looking for answers to mysteries both large and small—Are UFOs real? Where do my socks disappear to?—many would argue that the true value of a mystery lies not in its resolution, but rather in the curiosity and wonder it may inspire. As science pushes relentlessly onward in its quest to know all there is to know, there seems to be less and less curiosity in the world. Are there really fewer mysteries left to solve? Or does our curiosity help us discover new mysteries? Probably a bit of both. To fully engage with a mystery, one must perform a curious balancing act between faith and skepticism; faith that there is a mystery to solve and skepticism to temper the quest. Whatever your reason for reading this book—curiosity, boredom, skepticism or just because it was next to the magazine rack at the supermarket—I hope that these mysteries will inspire in you the spark of possibility.

–Geordie Telfer
Toronto, February 2012

MYSTERIOUS PLACES

Chapter One

The Peterborough Petroglyphs

~

In 1954, some prospectors were poking around in the woods near Peterborough. They were searching for valuable mineral deposits but discovered something else altogether. Making their way through a patch of thick underbrush, they came across a broad shelf of marble rising up through the earth

Alien figure: This vaguely extraterrestrial-looking entity is one of the 900 figures inscribed on the monolithic marble shelf that is the foundation of the Peterborough Petroglyphs.

~

and foliage. On it were hundreds upon hundreds of petro-glyphs—pictures carved into the rock by unknown hands, long, long ago. There were pictures of animals, people and strange figures with long necks and sun-like symbols for heads.

Although they didn't yet know it, the prospectors had stumbled across the largest surviving gallery of rock art in Ontario. The initial estimate was that there were about 90 pictographs on the broad, flat rock face, but experts soon determined that there were actually 900 separate images incised into the hard stone. With a surface area of several hundred square metres, the monolithic block of white marble was covered in

Female figure: The dark, vertical seam and its teardrop centre represent natural indentations in the rock that have been directly incorporated into the artwork, here representing a woman's womb.

~

artwork by long-dead hands. In many cases, natural features of the rock had been incorporated into the artwork carved into and around them.

Almost as soon as the petroglyphs were discovered, speculation began about their purpose. They would likely have been created by members of the Algonquin First Nation, but upon consulting with modern-day Algonquins, it was discovered that no tradition of rock painting had survived into the present. And though many locals, both First Nations and otherwise, had been aware of the stone images since the 1920s, no one knew what their meaning was. In the 1950s and '60s, one of the assumptions about comparable rock art, such as that in the caves at Lascaux, France, was that its creators were trying to exert influence over the things shown in the pictures. This supposed influence might manifest itself as success in the hunt, presumably in killing the animals shown the pictures, or perhaps even as influence over other people, if any human figures were represented. Another, less-fanciful notion was that rock art told a story, preserving an account of actual events for future generations. Less popular was the idea that then, as now, people created art simply for the act of creation, in effect "for something to do."

But the Peterborough Petroglyphs present something of a mystery if interpreted in any of these ways. To start with, the idea that the petroglyphs were created simply as artistic expression is problematic because marble is incredibly hard. The notion of Algonquin artisans painstakingly scraping away at hard stone, presumably with an even harder stone such as gneiss, just for something to do seems like a bit of a stretch, especially when much of their time would have been taken up with the struggle to survive. For purely artistic pursuits, the Algonquin are known to have used materials that were more easily worked than stone—birchbark, wood and, later, leather.

The idea that figures and symbols cut into the rock are meant to represent actual events is also problematic. Many of the figures, such as those shown in this chapter, are so fantastic that they clearly do not represent real animals or people, nor do they follow any kind of cohesive sequence that might allow an observer to construct a narrative or story. Most Algonquin clans were named after animals—for example, bear, eagle or beaver—and to represent the lineage of a family or the families in a given area, the Algonquin carved their famous totem poles. Through groupings of different totem animals, totem poles recorded the different families that comprised a community. This "family tree" may also have symbolically (or even practically) helped to promote exogamy—the practice of marrying non-relatives to keep the gene pool strong. Totem poles, then, chronicled actual events, after a fashion, but were constructed from wood. If the Peterborough Petroglyphs were meant to record events that had really happened, why switch to the much more difficult medium of stone?

Finally, there is the idea that the Peterborough Petro-glyphs were created to somehow influence the animals and fig-ures drawn there. Again, though, the figures are so fantastic that

THE PETERBOROUGH PETROGLYPHS

it is difficult to see what the hoped-for outcome might have been. However, the idea of the petroglyphs being associated with some sort of spiritual undertaking or process may not be far off the mark.

~

Before the arrival of Europeans, the Algonquin First Nation was spread over much of the eastern half of North America. It was not, however, a nation in the modern sense of the word; rather, the Algonquin First Nation comprised far-flung individuals, families and seasonal communities united by a common language and shared spiritual beliefs. The First Nations now known as the Ojibwa and the Ottawa spoke the Algonquin language, and though it differed from region to region, it was universal enough that speakers from different areas could make themselves understood to one another.

Their shared spiritual beliefs centred around the concept of *manitou*, the spirit-energy present in everything—people, animals, birds, trees, rocks and water. The force of *manitou* is stronger in some places and things than in others—cliffs and large outcroppings of rock, especially those with fissures and cracks, were (and still are) regarded as sacred places that may be doors to the spirit world.

As has already been mentioned, most Algonquin families were named after totem animals, but quite separate from that is the idea of a guardian spirit. Whereas a family's totem animal essentially represents a surname, an individual's spirit

Shaman: This figure likely represents a shaman (medicine man, healer, mystic or priest). The meaning of the pointed headgear and the paddle-like accoutrement is lost to history.

~

guide helps to aid and define that person in his or her day-to-day dealings with other people and the surrounding world—it shapes one's worldview significantly. The only way to acquire a spirit guide is to undertake a vision quest—fasting in solitude and possibly ingesting hallucinogens—until a vision appears that reveals one's spirit guide, which is typically a real or imagined animal, a celestial body or a spirit. Ideally, a vision quest should be carried out at a sacred place where *manitou* is strongly present, such as a large outcropping of stone or a rocky plateau.

The monolithic shelf of white marble on which the Peterborough Petroglyphs are incised bears all the hallmarks of a sacred site even without its remarkable works of art. *Manitou* would be present there. Moreover, the rock itself has deep fissures, cracks and other openings and markings that represent connections to the spirit world, giving it an extra fascination for the spiritually inclined. Some observers also report that, at certain times of the year, the sound of underground water can be heard emanating from the main crevice, and it sometimes strongly resembles a whispered cacophony of human voices, all speaking a language that is, of course, unintelligible to human ears. These characteristics earned the area its local name *Kinomagewapkong*, "The Teaching Rocks."

In the late 1960s, a comprehensive study of the Peterborough rock art was undertaken, and it was at that time that the number of observable figures was expanded from 90 to 900. It was also then that scholars formed the theory about the petroglyphs that is widely accepted today—the pictures show images that were seen during the vision quests of countless individuals who are now known to us only through the marks they left behind on a massive slab of rock. This would explain why the tough medium of stone was chosen—to more permanently record the most important spiritual experience a person might have in life. This theory also explains why so many of the figures show what appear to be divine beings, shamans or otherworldly creatures. What other reason would there be to chip and scrape away at a sacred site than to record a spiritual experience? It also explains the non-sequential profusion of individual figures and symbols. This interpretation makes the Peterborough Petroglyphs even more fascinating and enigmatic. Although we can never know for sure, how compelling to think that now, hundreds of years later, we can gaze through a window in time to share in a transcendent moment of spiritual revelation from long, long ago.

The Peterborough Petroglyphs are one of the few mysteries chronicled in this book that you can experience for yourself. The surrounding area, which is of great natural beauty, has been designated Petroglyphs Provincial Park. In the 1980s, a museum and interpretive centre was constructed around the vast marble bed on which the mysterious figures dance. A large, glass building now protects them from the elements and lets visitors get close without causing damage. There, you can look back in time to judge for yourself, perhaps sharing in the vision before you. Or you may even hear the burble of distant waters, spirit voices whispering their secrets for you to hear. In the end, the greatest gift of the Teaching Rocks may not be the visions they have sparked, but rather the wonder and sense of mystery they continue to inspire.

Chapter Two

The Serpent Mound

~

Truth be known, the so-called Serpent Mound in Peterborough isn't all that mysterious. However, it does cast a long and mysterious shadow, not least for its snaky-sounding name, which, though apt, isn't really accurate. What the Serpent Mound does have going for it is notoriety—it is the most famous and best documented of Ontario's handful of ancient Aboriginal burial mounds, which are scattered across the province like pebbles flung from the palm of some long-ago giant.

Two thousand years ago, long before the arrival of Europeans, the forebears of today's First Nations populated the central-eastern portion of North America. They were not a single unified society, but rather many separate communities and cultures that have been lumped together by modern scholars because these groups were active at the same time. Since their languages and customs are largely lost to us, there are no clues as to what these groups might have called themselves in their native tongues, and archaeologists have instead named them after the locations of early dig sites. The Adena people were prolific mound builders and created mounds sometimes for ceremonial rituals, but largely for burial rites. They flourished from 1000 BCE to 200 BCE, with the present-day U.S. state of Ohio as a locus of archaeological evidence. Following the Adena was the Hopewell group, which was more advanced and widely dispersed. The Hopewell flourished from about 200 BCE to 500 CE and also spread into present-day Canada, primarily in and around the Great Lakes. They, too, built mounds for burial rites and other ceremonies.

Ontario's oldest burial mounds are thought to originate in the Hopewell era, and the Peterborough Serpent Mound is one of these. It is situated on a high point overlooking Rice Lake. There, sheltered from the winds coming off the lake by a small copse of trees along the shore, rests the main Serpent Mound. It is surrounded by eight smaller mounds, none of which is snake shaped. Drawn in 1897 by David Boyle, the central mound looked like this:

Central Serpent Mound, 1897: David Boyle, the man who named the Serpent Mound, admitted that he was influenced by knowledge of other "effigy mounds." Did he embellish the mound's actual shape to make it look more serpentine?

When the Royal Ontario Museum excavated the site from 1957 to 1960, the central mound was rendered thus:

Central Serpent Mound, 1957–60: Has the mound's serpentine shape been lost over the years or was it never there to begin with?

It is impossible to know whether David Boyle, the man who first investigated the site in 1897, embellished the actual shape of the mound to make it more "snaky"—he did, after all, dub one of the other mounds "the Egg"—or whether, in the following 60 years, other diggers (of whom there was abundant evidence) gradually destroyed its original serpentine outline. Boyle did admit that he was influenced by knowledge of North America's only recognized "effigy mound," a mound that had been deliberately constructed to resemble a creature or thing— the famous and much larger Serpent Mound in Adams County, Ohio. The Ohio Serpent Mound is 382 metres long, with an elaborately spiralled "tail," a winding "body" and a "head" that seems to be devouring a large egg or possibly the head of a human. While the U.S. boasts one or two other much smaller effigy mounds, the fact remains that what many people are eager to romantically dub "serpent mounds" could more aptly be described simply as wiggly hills that bear little or no resemblance to an actual snake.

The Peterborough Serpent Mound is about 50 metres long and 7.6 metres wide, with an average height of about 1.5 metres. The surrounding mounds, which are roughly round or oval, range from 7 to 14.6 metres long (or wide, depending on their proportions) with heights ranging from 0.4 to 1.6 metres. If the Serpent Mound ever had a bulbous "head" or pointed "tail" as shown in Boyle's drawing, both have long since vanished. In its present-day form, the mound could, with some justification, be called a "caterpillar" or "fat salamander."

Upon investigation, the Serpent Mound and its satellites were discovered to be burial grounds dating from the Hopewell era. The central mound contained the skeletal remains of 25 people, most of whom were adults, though there were some adolescents and at least one infant. To judge from the various layers of earth, the burials took place many years apart. The earliest were the "primary" burials, individuals whose remains had been placed in the mound soon after their deaths. These bodies were arranged on their sides in a loose fetal position, with their arms and legs tucked up as if they were curling up under the blankets at night. The bodies that comprised the primary burials were interred slightly below ground level, suggesting that they were among the first to be placed there, with the rest of the mound eventually being constructed over them. Some bodies had been cremated where they lay, while others had not. Some were buried individually, whereas others were in pairs. The bones of other individuals—"secondary" burials—had apparently been interred long after their deaths. These were piles of loose bones carefully arranged, generally in the higher and therefore more recent strata of the mound. Of the graves excavated, 21 were concentrated in the eastern half of the Serpent Mound, toward the "head." Most of the western half of the mound has not been excavated, but a smaller dig toward the "tail" revealed four additional graves.

The primary burials, in the lower layers of the mound, often had small objects placed with the bodies, including copper-foil and silver beads, ceramics, the teeth, jaws and mandibles of bears, wolves and other creatures, as well as shell discs pierced in the middle as though they had been threaded on a bracelet or necklace. There were also stone arrow- or spearheads. Only two of the surrounding mounds have been excavated, but these yielded all or part of 49 human skeletons.

A carbon-dating comparison of soil samples from the opposite ends of the Serpent Mound produced telling results—the eastern end (the "head") dated from about 128 CE, whereas the western end (the "tail") dated from nearly 200 years later, 302 CE. This could suggest that the burials began as a single, shallow mound at the "head," with subsequent burials added on top, eventually extending westward as generation after generation buried their dead. If this is what happened, it considerably weakens the notion that the Serpent Mound was deliberately constructed as the effigy of a snake—it is difficult to imagine eight generations conspiring over nearly 200 years to bury their ancestors in such a shape, especially when no other evidence of true effigy mounds has been found in Canada, much less Ontario. It is also worth remembering that an excavation of the Serpent Mound in Ohio revealed that no human remains or artifacts were buried in it, suggesting that it was simply a large and elaborate expression of worship or even simple creativity. What seems most likely is that the Ontario Serpent Mound's unusual shape grew from a series of additions to the one original mound, or perhaps two or more mounds eventually ran together, an idea that finds some support in the observable overlap of two of the smaller satellite mounds.

Questions, of course, remain. Why should some of the community's members have been buried in the main Serpent Mound, whereas others were consigned to the satellite mounds? Were those in the Serpent Mound part of a particularly influential family, clan or tribe? If the secondary burials were bodies interred long after their deaths, where were they buried before? Why weren't these individuals buried in the Serpent Mound when they died? Could their bodies have been discovered when new graves were being dug and then reburied? This would lend credence to the idea that the mound's unusual proportions come from the gradual growth of several smaller mounds into one big one, with bones disturbed by digging being carefully arranged and respectfully reinterred.

However, the mere fact of knowing something's purpose need not eliminate the sense of wonder that comes from contemplating it. After all, there is no great mystery about, for example, the Eiffel Tower, but people are still moved and amazed by it. The Serpent Mound invites our curiosity and wonder simply because it is a place of ancestors. Our forebears, whose day-to-day lives we can never know, rest there. Just as in a cemetery or any other burial place, there are untold stories and sleeping secrets. The Serpent Mound inspires a sense of mystery, not because its purpose is shrouded in obscurity (its purpose is quite clear), but rather because it connects us to the past, to a time when magic, mystery and wonder could be a part of everyday life.

GHOSTS AND
THE PARANORMAL

Chapter Three

The Baldoon Mystery

~

From 1828 to 1831, the McDonald family of Baldoon, near Chatham, found their lives and livelihood ruined by an ongoing series of poltergeist phenomena that was witnessed by scores of their neighbours and fellow settlers in the area. The author of the account upon which most of this chapter is based was Neil T. McDonald, a child of the family, born around 1821. Decades after the events occurred, he sought out those old enough to recall them and obtained a series of sworn statements that are remarkably consistent in their recounting of the strange occurrences that follow.

Aside from its famous haunting, Baldoon is probably best known as the site of a disastrous attempt at colonization by Lord Alexander Selkirk in 1804. This well-meaning but utterly incompetent Scottish laird sent scores of his countrymen to their deaths by shipping them to Canada in order to populate harsh, inhospitable landscapes that already had people living on them. Selkirk high-handedly annexed land set aside for a First Nations reserve and, instead, gave it to his impoverished colonists. As we shall see, this may have had a direct bearing on the events that followed.

Off the St. Clair River in Baldoon lies a small tributary that the French named *Channel Écarte*. It was there that settler Daniel McDonald built a sturdy log house and raised a brood of nine children. When Daniel's eldest son, John, was ready to marry, a second log-frame house was built close to the main family home. It was primarily in this second house, but soon all over the farm, that strange occurrences began to take place.

The women of the McDonald family were able weavers and, one day, they were in the barn separating flax fibres to be used in weaving cloth. Several poles had been slung across the rafters of the barn and a cloth spread across the poles; in this improvised loft, the flax fibres could be kept safely out of harm's way once they had been separated. That afternoon, all present were surprised when one of the poles fell from the rafters. They put it back and thought no more of the incident until, a few minutes later, another of the poles slipped and crashed to the ground. The women searched the barn from top to bottom for the mischievous squirrel or other animal that was surely causing the disturbances, but they found none, and after a third pole fell in their midst, they retreated to the farmhouse.

In the house, no sooner had the women settled down to their many other domestic chores than there was a crash from one of the windows and a *bullet* fell at their feet. It was followed by a second bullet, then a veritable hail of them. The bullets smashed through the windows, then lost their momentum and simply dropped to the floor. Terrified and puzzled, the women hurried to the nearby home of a neighbour. Meanwhile, a family acquaintance, Mr. L.A. McDougald, called at the McDonald house and became alarmed when he saw the bullet holes in the windows. He also hurried to the neighbour's house and, finding the women there, persuaded them to return with him. Back at the McDonald home, there were lead balls the size of musket shot all over the floor.

These mysterious projectiles would continue to plague the family, with McDougald later writing, "I have been present when balls came through the windows. I and others have picked them up, putting a private mark upon them and thrown them into the river, and in a short time, the same balls so marked would come back through the window. At other times, stones would come wet, as if they were just out of the bed of the river."

Another witness, Re-Nah-Sewa, from one of the surrounding First Nations settlements wrote, "I saw the balls come through the windows and I would tie them in a small bag…and in a few minutes we would examine the bag, and to our surprise, not a ball would be left in it." Still other witnesses swore they had seen the lead balls come through the windows, picked them up, marked them and thrown them into the river where it was about 10 metres deep, only to have identically marked balls appear again in the house.

But the bullets were just the beginning. Nine days after the poles in the barn had fallen and the first bullets had come through the windows, John McDonald and his wife were asleep in bed when they awoke at midnight to the sound of footsteps, as though several people were marching through the kitchen. Roused by a cry of alarm from one of their children, who slept in a room just off the kitchen, John McDonald jumped out of bed and flung open the kitchen door. The sounds immediately stopped, and nothing in the kitchen was out of place.

However, this was not the last time one of the McDonald children would be disturbed by the malevolent force. One of the infants was sleeping peacefully in a cradle, when, according to witness William S. Fleury, "the cradle began to rock fearfully and no one was near it. They thought it would throw the child out, so two men undertook to stop it but could not, still, a third took hold but stop it they could not. Some of the party said, 'Let's test this,' so they put the Bible in the cradle and it stopped instantly."

Alas, the poor baby could get no peace. Another witness, Captain Lewis Bennet, a British army officer, reported that one day while he was at the McDonald's house, the baby was asleep in the cradle when the child suddenly began to scream. Upon investigation, a large, hot stone was discovered under the baby's bedclothes. The stone was so hot that when it was thrown into the water, the water hissed. The same stone reappeared several more times in the room in the following minutes.

If it seems odd that so many people were around, there was good reason—the case was famous. Friends, acquaintances and complete strangers came from far and wide to see what they could see at the McDonald residence. More often than not, friends of the family were present because they wanted to be able to lend assistance if anything went wrong. The many curiosity seekers who came by simply wanted to see something unusual—and they were seldom disappointed.

One visitor who hoped to see something strange was Neil Campbell, who was boastfully proclaiming his disbelief in the supernatural when a large stone flew through a window and struck him on the chest. After the incident in which bullets shattered all the windows, the McDonalds replaced the glass with sturdy planks of wood, but the lead balls and stones somehow managed to penetrate these; they left no marks on the wood, seemingly floating right through it. For the most part, though, it was the family's everyday possessions, the tools of their daily chores, that were most often animated by the unpredictable force. Witness M.L. Burnham wrote, "At this time, everything in and about the house seemed under the influence, nothing in the house could be kept in place; the shovel and tongs would run about the floor as would other things about the house. The cooking was done by a large fireplace, and it was extremely difficult to keep anything upon the fire. The old Dutch oven would empty itself, making it extremely hard to get enough material cooked to satisfy their hunger."

Allen M. McDonald, one of the children living in the house at the time, testified, "I saw an auger [a long, old-fashioned drill bit], which was hanging on a nail, blow across the room, and strike the bed post with such force that it coiled around the post…" Of one visit to the McDonald's, Mrs. S. Stewart said, "I had only been seated for a few minutes when the frying pan hopped out from a small place between the corner of the room and a large cupboard, and fell to the floor about twelve feet [3.6 metres] from the place from which it started." One skeptical neighbour, Thomas Burgess, paid a visit, and almost as soon as he entered the house, "the two wooden andirons that were in the fireplace rose up to the ceiling and one lodged on each side of the house."

One night, one of the McDonald boys asked family friend L.A. McDougald if he would stay with him in his room because the child was frightened of what might happen. McDougald wrote, "We retired to an upper chamber, but not to rest, for the bed rocked all night with a gentle undulating motion of a wave of the sea. My companion told me that this was a common occurrence, and they had become so used to it that they did not mind it much."

McDougald seems to have been privy to many of the strangest events of the Baldoon mystery. One day, upon entering the house with McDonald daughter Jane, McDougald saw that "Every article of furniture in the house was piled in a kind of window, which extended cornerwise across the room. A space of a couple of feet was left in the centre of the pile and the family Bible was opened and turned down on the floor." Amazingly, the farmhouse even levitated off its foundation, rising up into the air, first at one end, and then the other, much to the consternation of those inside.

Other strange events were considered comparatively mundane as the apparent haunting dragged on. A bar of soap shot across the room and smacked one of the children in the back. A knife with a 25-centimetre steel blade hurled itself across the room and buried the entire length of its blade in the mortar of the wall. Dishes flew out of cupboards. The kettle floated about the room frequently and sometimes with great force—on one occasion, the lid came off with such violence that it left a half-centimetre gash in the window casing. Guns spontaneously fired themselves. Vessels of water would float around the room and empty themselves. Empty shoes would walk around of their own volition. A visiting peddler's coins went missing, only to reappear, rap on the window and then drop into his lap where he sat at the table. A loaf of bread floated jauntily through the air. Coins dropped from the ceiling. Flying stones knocked out door panels. The lead weights of the McDonalds' fishing net would detach themselves, disappear and then drop from the ceiling inside the house, dripping wet as though they had just come out of the river. Pieces of furniture crashed about of their own accord, and once a chair floated into the air amid the startled cries of its distraught occupant. In one of the most frequently recounted instances, multiple witnesses swore that they had witnessed Mrs. McDonald give the family dog a pot to lick, whereupon either the pot or its ladle began whacking the dog on both sides of its face. The poor beast fled, apparently turning up several weeks later in Michigan, though how this came to be known is unclear.

There was more to follow. Soon, mysterious fires began erupting throughout the house, often in places where it seemed no human agency could possibly reach, such as *inside* sealed sections of wall. L.A. McDougald described what happened when his father and another man volunteered to watch over the house:

> As they sat talking they saw smoke coming from a small closet and on examining, they found a fire nicely built upon the floor with corn cobs and coals. There was but one entrance to the closet and no one could have gone in without their knowledge. They extinguished it but soon smoke began to come from the wall. They tore away the laths and plaster and there found another fire similar to the one in the closet. And so it continued for some time, as fast as they quenched the fire in one place it broke out in another...

Eyewitnesses also described fires that occurred with baffling frequency. William Fleury wrote:

> I saw the house take fire up stairs in ten different places at once. There were plenty to watch the fires, as people came from all parts of the United States and Canada to see for themselves. Not less than from twenty to fifty men were there all the time.

Neil Campbell said he had seen the house catch fire 50 times in one day and had helped to douse the flames each time. On a different occasion, a local First Nations man, Solomon Par-Tar-Sung, passed by the house upon returning from hunting and, seeing no less than 30 men there struggling to contain the fires, lent a hand to help. He later wrote:

> *It had been set on fire thirty times in less than three hours. A small coal of fire, about the size of a hickory nut would drop in any part of the house and a flame would kindle immediately. There was no fire used in the house and we had water ready to put on the coals the instant they dropped. It would take fire on the wet floor the same as if it were oil, until it was drenched with water.*

One morning, after several days of these unexplained fires, John McDonald's home burned to the ground. No one was injured, but now the beleaguered family had to find a new place to live. They were taken in by a series of kind-hearted neighbours, but the terrifying occurrences followed them. Several broken windows later, they eventually settled with John's father, Daniel (who is sometimes referred to as David), in his house, close to the one that had burned down. The disturbances soon followed them here as well, with the customary lead balls, flying stones and moving furniture. Now another blight came upon the McDonalds as their livestock started to die off. Horses dropped dead in their stalls, a pair of prize oxen spontaneously keeled over in the field, hens died after laying eggs and the pigs slowly succumbed to a mysterious wasting sickness.

Eventually, Daniel, the patriarch, along with son John and his family were reduced to living in a canvas tent situated between the two homes. But even bags of clothes rescued from either house would begin to smoulder if left alone too long. Garments soaked with water as a safeguard against fire would spontaneously ignite as soon as they were hung out to dry. Not long after this, the barn caught fire. As flames consumed the wooden structure, several witnesses reported seeing a large, unfamiliar, black dog seated atop the burning building. One woman said she had seen the dog run up a plank that was leaning against the burning building. It sat there happily amid the flames and smoke, looking down upon the frantic efforts to extinguish the blaze. When people began lobbing burning sticks at the animal, seemingly convinced it was an agent of the evil forces acting upon the McDonalds, the dog bared its teeth at them but otherwise sat resolutely as the building beneath it burned, eventually disappearing into thin air before the startled onlookers.

At about this time, an odd incident occurred that only became significant once the haunting ended. An elderly woman (to judge from later statements, she may have been of First Nations heritage) lived nearby with her sons in a structure known as the "Long Low Log House." She wanted to hire John McDonald's aunt to weave a carpet for her, but the aunt told her that with all the calamities afoot in the McDonald homestead, she could neither undertake nor promise to complete the work. The old woman, with considerable self-assurance, said that the household would be untroubled by disturbances while the weaving was being done. With some doubts, the aunt accepted the work and, for the few weeks that it took her to complete the carpet, peace reigned in the house, only for the chaos to resume once the project was finished.

There now enters into the plot a figure whose business in the story is all at once praiseworthy, unfortunate and rather funny. A nearby schoolmaster named Robert Barker fancied himself an expert in the supernatural. Hearing of the queer goings-on at the McDonald farm, Barker decided that this was a good time to put his arcane knowledge of the dark arts to use. He planned to employ his expertise in magic to rid the property of the evil spirits that infested it. Really, all he did was nail a placard above the door that read in large letters:

I COMMAND YOU TROUBLESOME SPIRIT TO LEAVE THIS HOUSE

IN THE NAME OF THE FATHER, THE SON AND THE HOLY GHOST.

Barker also nailed a horseshoe above the door. The troublesome spirit took absolutely no notice, but the local authorities did—they arrested Barker for practising witchcraft. He was locked up in jail for six months until his trial, which caused him no end of worry because he had a family to support. When the time for his trial finally arrived, the court determined that no action would be taken against him, and the unfortunate Barker was released with a stern warning not to practise witchcraft again. Now a broken man, he reportedly moved with his family to the U.S.

Shortly after this, John McDonald learned of Dr. John F. Troyer (1753–1842), a herbalist and self-styled witch hunter who lived in Norfolk County, about 130 kilometres away, a couple of days on horseback. McDonald and a companion undertook the journey, enduring many strange sounds, sights and other ill omens as they rode along. Upon reaching Dr. Troyer's log cabin (likely located at present-day Troyer's Flats, about three kilometres east of Port Rowan), they described the odd manifestations as Troyer listened intently. Troyer then introduced the men to his 15-year-old daughter (not named in any of the accounts, so we shall call her Troyer *fille*). Troyer *fille* was sallow and frail, with a strange, faraway look in her eyes—Troyer told them that she was a seer. Troyer *fille* listened to McDonald's tale and then announced that she would consult the "moonstone," a stone found by her father that enhanced her "second sight" and acted as a sort of crystal ball, or viewer, for her visions. After consulting the moonstone, she confidently announced that another of the McDonald's outbuildings had just burned down. The men checked their watches, and later, upon their return to Chatham, found that the young woman was correct. Troyer *fille* next described the old woman who lived with her sons in the Long Low Log House. Was it possible that the parcel of land owned by the McDonalds was coveted by these people? John McDonald recalled that yes, they had wanted to buy it, but he had refused to sell. The girl next asked if, among the McDonald's geese, there was a bird with a black head and part of one wing also black? After a moment's thought, McDonald recalled, that yes, there was such a goose, but he had always thought it part of his flock and paid it no mind. Troyer *fille* then announced that his problems would be solved if he shot the goose with a silver bullet. Outlandish as this sounded, the girl had described the situation so accurately that McDonald was inclined to do whatever she said if there was a chance it would end the terrifying manifestations that plagued him and his family. With many thanks, McDonald and his companion set out for home.

When he got there, McDonald asked his children if they knew the goose with the black markings (presumably, tending to the geese was one of the children's chores). They replied that yes, they knew it well, for it was always noisy and temperamental. After fashioning a silver bullet at a neighbour's house, McDonald loaded his gun and gathered witnesses for what he was about to do. The little procession walked to the bank of the river where the geese were allowed to run free. McDonald pointed out the goose with the black markings to his baffled audience, then took aim and fired. He wounded the goose's wing, and the bird uttered a strangled sound that suggested a human voice and took cover among the reeds along the riverbank. Next, John McDonald walked over to the Long Low Log Cabin and entered. He found the elderly matriarch sitting in her chair, glowering at him balefully and making a very poor job of trying to conceal her broken arm.

After this, the manifestations ceased. Although it was a long, hard haul, the McDonald clan slowly rebuilt their farm. Crops grew once more. New livestock was procured and did not mysteriously die. The strange fires ceased to burn. Bullets and kettles no longer sailed through the air of their own volition. The family, at last, could get a decent night's sleep. The old woman of the Long Low Log House did not trouble the McDonalds any more, but she was said to be wracked with pains from that day forward, unable to sit comfortably without terrible pangs shooting agonizingly through her body. On her deathbed, she supposedly asked to see John McDonald, but her sons would not deliver the message to him.

We shall, of course, never know what truly happened during those years so long ago. Certainly, a belief in the supernatural was likely much more prevalent in rural Ontario of the early 19th century than it is today. It is important to note that the sworn statements collected by Neil T. McDonald (son of John) were taken *50 years* after the events described. It is also odd that many of the accounts agree so exactly—one would expect the eyewitnesses to differ a bit more and the stories to have more contradictory elements. It is almost as though, after 50 years of hearing one another describe the events over and over again, the witnesses had arrived at a common version of what happened, complete with similar phrases.

On the other hand, it is surely too much to believe that an entire community, bolstered by countless visitors from afar, confabulated the whole thing. Clearly *something* happened—we just don't know what. Modern interpretations of the mystery are probably correct in supposing that some sort of land dispute was at the heart of it. Significantly, the statements of the two First Nations eyewitnesses, Re-Nah-Sewa and Solomon Par-Tar-Sung, seem to confirm this.

Re-Nah-Sewa recalled:

The trouble was caused in this way—J.T. McDonald purchased a piece of land which the disturbers wanted and these are the steps they took to have revenge on him. I saw his corn and it did not grow more than a foot high that year and his crops were all destroyed by them. We called them wild Indians in our language and we believe they made their abode in the prairie southeast of the house on the farm. We were aware of their doings and tried to tell him what we knew about them, but could not understand each other's language.

Solomon Par-Tar-Sung remembered:

We are satisfied that what you call witchcraft, we call wild Indians, and that they have their abode in a small prairie on the same farm, but could not be seen at any time....We are satisfied that all this trouble was that John T. McDonald purchased the same farm that the wild Indians wanted, and to have revenge on him, they took these steps to destroy his property.

Neither man specifies whether the "wild Indians" used earthly or supernatural means to achieve their ends, but the idea of a land dispute with neighbouring First Nations does not seem unlikely. There is anecdotal evidence to suggest that the area was home to a sacred medicine lodge, and that following the disastrous arrival of Selkirk in 1804, conflicts became frequent as white settlers impinged more and more on "Indian land." And coincidentally or not, the name "Long Low Log House" does conjure the image of a lodge of some sort. It is possible that the Baldoon Mystery has, at its core, the age-old conflict that has come to define Canada—the theft of sacred Aboriginal lands by European settlers.

Chapter Four

The Spectral Lights of Cornwall

~

I nvestigating a haunting that occurred more than 150 years ago is difficult enough, but searching for clues when the haunted house is under several metres of water presents another level of difficulty altogether. With the construction of the St. Lawrence Seaway in the 1950s, many small settlements were inundated "full fathom five," as Shakespeare put it. Among these was the homestead known in the 19th century as Marsh's Point on the outskirts of a thriving little community called Milles-Roches.

Until the 1830s, Milles-Roches was located on a large headland that stuck out into the St. Lawrence River. But starting in 1834, with the construction of the Cornwall Canal, the village was transformed into an island by the new waterway that separated it from the mainland by several metres. Milles-Roches was now inaccessible except via a dripping underwater tunnel that connected it to the mainland. The canal also severed Marsh's Point from the mainland, as well as from Milles-Roches. It was now an island that could only be reached through the subaqueous passage known as the "Milles-Roches culvert."

The house on Marsh's Point had been built decades earlier in a picturesque little grove of hickory trees. It had a pointed roof with steep, sloping sides, and its solitary placement on its own small island gave it a still, ghostly air. The house's occupants were Clara Marsh, aged 60, and her mother, 80, who was only ever referred to as "Granny" Marsh. The women rarely left their house except when they braved the seeping tunnel to go into town for supplies.

One night, in the autumn of 1845, a farmer was walking along the edge of the canal on the mainland side. He happened to look toward Marsh's Point and was surprised to see a number of moving lights near the house, as though several people were carrying lanterns about. He assumed that the Marsh women were either gravely ill or injured or had some other misfortune befall them that required help from the neighbours. The next morning, the farmer called at the house to express his sympathy or condolences, whichever might be required. Imagine his surprise when he found that both Granny and Clara Marsh were fine, and furthermore, that they had no idea a party of lantern bearers had been swarming around their house the night before—in fact, the notion quite amused them.

Sightings of the ghostly lights continued, with more and more people seeing them until finally all of the Marshes' neighbours had, at one time or another, been witness to the strange illuminations that floated around the old farmhouse. After the Marsh women themselves finally saw the lights, they asked nearby farming families to keep watch on their property for any strange "doings." The inhabitants of the entire countryside rose to the occasion, all eager to solve the mystery. The watchers organized themselves into pairs and set up nightly patrols on Marsh's Point, vigilantly peering into the darkness as the two women slept inside the house.

One of most puzzling aspects of the whole affair was that observers on the mainland often saw things happening near the house that the night watchers who were actually *at* the house were completely unaware of. One night, people keeping watch from the far side of the canal swore they saw a red-hot stove in front of the house, with several figures carrying pans of bread back and forth between the glowing oven and the surrounding darkness. But the Marsh's Point watchers who were on the property that night said they hadn't seen anything of the sort, neither phantom oven nor spectral bakers. Subsequent inquiries showed that no oven or stove matching the one observed could be found anywhere in the house or on the property.

However, people in the house and on the immediate property also reported strange goings-on. The Marshes began to hear strange sounds in the disused sections of the rambling old house. Although the so-called ghosts never invaded Granny and Clara's actual living quarters, loud noises began to emanate from the darkened rooms and passages that the Marsh family had occupied during the house's heyday. The two women were quite frightened but could not be persuaded to leave. Eventually, they appear to have simply grown used to the noisy disturbances, which did them no harm besides startling them out of their slumbers.

One of the Milles-Roches locals was an old soldier who had fought with the Duke of Wellington when his troops defeated Napoleon at Waterloo in 1814. One night, this hardened old campaigner and another local were keeping watch inside the house when a human silhouette popped up in front of an open window. The soldier commanded the intruder to stand up and identify him- or herself. The figure nodded but began to move away, so the old soldier repeated the command. Getting no response, the Waterloo veteran raised his rifle and fired at the figure, which collapsed to the ground outside the house. When the two men ran outside to look, neither of them could find anything at the spot where they had seen the figure fall.

By far, the most frequently seen and most baffling phenomenon was the ongoing presence of large numbers of floating lights. Sometimes visible only from the mainland, but other times also quite apparent from the house, the dancing lights tended to appear in groups. On one occasion, the lights appeared to gather themselves into an enormous formation over the house, swinging back and forth in a straight line, like a pendulum describing an arc. Another time, they were seen to run along the ground in a line until they reached a tree, whereupon the lights climbed the trunk and scattered prettily among the branches, apparently playing hide and seek, like so many fireflies. Sometimes the lights' movements seemed random and rather playful, while at other times they appeared to show purpose and deliberation. One night, as observers looked on from the mainland, a cluster of lights gathered on the Marsh's Point side by the water of the canal. There they hovered, except for one of their number that struck out across the canal, very close to the surface of the water. To the amazement of the onlookers, the single light sped across the water until it reached the other side of the canal some distance away, then shot up into the branches of an immense tree and seemed to dart around as though looking about from this high vantage point. Next, the light descended, crossed the canal again and appeared to be welcomed back to Marsh's Point by its waiting companions, which clustered around the light as though wanting to hear of any news or perhaps congratulate it on its bravery.

Writing 25 years later in the *New Dominion Monthly* in November 1869, a writer identified only as "J.H. McN." reported these events but expressed a great deal of skepticism about them, assuming the incidents to be greatly exaggerated accounts of some unexplained earthly phenomenon. Still, J.H. McN. did acknowledge the impracticality of the notion that it was all some sort of hoax intended to frighten the Marshes, writing that "the idea of a number of experts combining to work the machinery for effecting such results as those witnessed" was not merely unlikely, but impossible. The large number of witnesses certainly gives the alleged haunting a whiff of veracity, but the fact that people on the mainland reported things that were not seen by the observers at Marsh's Point suggests that some sort of mass delusion or hallucination may have been involved.

Certainly, the inhabitants of Milles-Roche had been greatly traumatized by the isolating effect that the Cornwall Canal had upon their community—it completely destroyed the economy of the little town along with the citizens' livelihoods. During the construction of the canal, local merchants and other town worthies had appealed to the provincial legislature to provide compensation for lost income and property, as well as for a series of bridges to be built to reconnect Milles-Roches to the mainland. Although some compensatory money was eventually forthcoming, Mille-Roches and Marsh's Point remained cut off from the mainland. Is it possible that the collective emotional strain combined with unknown environmental factors somehow produced a perceived mass haunting?

With the approach of winter, the strange events ceased. Neither the mysterious lights nor the strange sounds ever again troubled Granny and Clara Marsh. In subsequent years, the fortunes of the citizens of Milles-Roches improved. With the coming of the railway in the 1850s, the little town began to flourish once again. A paper mill opened in Milles-Roches in the early 1900s and eventually became the town's main industry. By the 1930s, it was a thriving community with many businesses and even a large public skating rink. But in the 1950s, the mill closed and the town's life began to ebb; the construction of the

St. Lawrence Seaway sealed its fate forever. Now submerged under 13 metres of water, Milles-Roches is one of Ontario's sunken ghost towns, sites lost to the deluge of diverted waters. With its many ruins, it is a popular site for scuba divers, so if you are truly keen to dig deeper into the Marsh's Point mystery, perhaps there, under the waves, you will find some ghostly glimmer of a clue.

Chapter Five

The Ghost of University College

~

To walk through the University of Toronto's downtown campus is to stroll through time itself. The buildings are a striking mixture of old, stately stone structures and modern curtains of shimmering glass and brutalist concrete. In the university's Morrison Hall Residence, a towering modern monolith, you will find the Café Reznikoff, named for

University College today: The Roundhouse at the extreme left of the photo is the site of the haunting.

~

the central character in the U of T's most enduring ghost story. Like the campus itself, the story's themes are a tug-of-war between old and new, façade and reality, the difference between words and actions.

Briefly, the story is this—as the construction of University College was nearing completion in 1859, two immigrant stonemasons, Ivan Reznikoff and Paul Diabolos, were working on the building. Both men were in love with the same woman. Diabolos convinced her to run away with him (along with all of Reznikoff's savings), but not before his rival learned of the plot and intervened. In the ensuing fight, jilted lover Reznikoff was killed, and his ghost haunted University College until his bones were discovered in 1890 and given a proper burial. Two stone gargoyles, still visible at University College, were supposedly carved by the competing paramours, each a grotesque parody of the other's features. Massive gashes in the oaken door of the Roundhouse are said to be the spot where Reznikoff swung his axe at Diabolos and missed. (The Roundhouse is a large, turret-like structure at the west end of the building. It was once a chemistry lab but is now known as Croft Chapter House.) This is where most accounts leave off, which is all very well, but a look at the origins of this story reveal a world far stranger and more remote than any ghost story, namely the city of Toronto in the mid-19th century.

If the previous paragraph, with its talk of gargoyles and gashes, has left you holding your breath in the hope that here, at last, is the ghost story you've been waiting for, replete with concrete evidence and documented proof, you probably shouldn't exhale quite yet. The story as we know it today stems from an eight-volume work, *Studies of Student Life*, written by U of T alumnus William James Loudon, whose family had a long connection with the university. Loudon was a prolific writer across a broad range of diverse topics. His *Studies of Student Life* was published from the early 1920s to the 1940s and recalled events that happened at least 60 years earlier. The Reznikoff ghost story appears in Volume 5, published in 1928. In its day, it may have been a light, breezy reminiscence of halcyon varsity life, but to a modern reader, Volume 5 is quite simply one of the strangest marriages of ink and paper ever to see the light of day. It is prefaced by two telling quotations and a disclaimer:

> *Nothing like a little judicious levity.*
>
> —Robert Louis Stevenson

> *The ghosts that walk at midnight, shrink*
> *Ere cockcrow to their haunts again:*
> *The things, that in the night we think,*
> *Are brushed, at morning, from the brain.*
>
> —Anon.

> *N.B.—This book has been specially written not only for those who lean, at times, upon the supernatural, but also for all those unbelievers, men of little faith, who grope about from day to day with outstretched hands and search*

in vain for some token of their own immortality. Its contents are to be taken with the proverbial grain of salt. [Author's emphasis]

Well, that's nice. W.J. Loudon's sentiment in the foregoing lines is basically that "everything you're about to read may or may not be true." One also suspects that the quote attributed to "Anon." is, in fact, by the author himself. Be that as it may, the book is a telling document of its time. For instance, a recurring theme is the disappearance of the "classical" curriculum—Greek and Latin—for one more in tune with the modern day. Loudon only half-jokingly describes the attitudes of relict Victorians who:

> *...laugh disdainfully at all those engaged in teaching the psycho branches of knowledge, sociology, the care of infants, childhood; and gaze with helpless eye on the march of Co-education, with its teas, dances, women's clubs, minstrel shows, hockey teams, swimming competitions, and other barbaric exhibitions: while they watch, with dismay, the slow but steady encroachment of women upon the field of mental and physical activities formerly occupied solely by men.*

Why am I telling you all this? Well, to provide some sort of provenance for what follows. The first two-thirds of the volume are taken up with a biography of one "John Smith." It is he who lays down the groundwork of the Reznikoff ghost story. Smith embodies the tug between old and new that lies at the centre of this tale; he arrives at University College a naïve country bumpkin hoping to become a minister but leaves a decade later having become a lawyer! When it comes time for Smith to join a fraternity, he joins not Phi Beta Epsilon or Alpha Delta Gamma—no, no—he joins the *Ku Klux Klan,* which in this rosy, nostalgic vision has nothing to do with racism, but with keeping up appearances. For instance, in one episode, the KKK fines Smith for wearing a cheap paper shirt collar when a more expensive cloth one would have better befitted his status as a member of their prestigious brotherhood. Loudon admits that "John Smith" is not the man's real name, but goes on to aver that after he graduated from U of T, Smith was eventually knighted (among several other dubious claims).

Another notable aspect of this narrative is its barely veiled enthusiasm for that totem of varsity life, alcohol. When John Smith arrives in Toronto, he is a simple farm boy, inexperienced in the ways of the world and innocent of Dionysian revels. By the end of the book, though, he is an enthusiastic tippler and may or may not have consumed more than an entire bottle of whisky by himself as he listens to Reznikoff's ghost recount its life and death. And with this, we are ready to proceed to the tale at hand. But bear in mind what we have learned so far:

1) The tale occurs in a time far removed from our own in outlook and mores;

2) The teller of the tale, by his own admission, consumed a staggering amount of whisky during the events he describes.

~

In the 1850s, Toronto was beginning to emerge from the period during which it had been known as "Muddy York." With a population of about 30,000, it was no longer a provincial backwater; rather, it was becoming recognized as a small but influential city, the seat of government in Upper Canada. After the so-called Great Fire of Toronto in 1849 (not to be confused with a 1904 fire also referred to by the same name), the city had embarked on a reconstruction boom that saw many fine new buildings rise from the ashes.

At that time, higher education in Canada was mired in a political conflict fought across a religious divide. King's College opened in 1843, but the endowment with which it was built was seen to be blatant government favouritism partial to the ruling Protestant clique known as the "Family Compact." In 1853, the University of Toronto Act paved the way for another educational endowment. To avoid the denominational firestorm that had plagued the King's College endowment, no less a luminary than John A. Macdonald (not yet Canada's first prime minister), advised the stakeholders to simply take the money and construct a building; he remarked that not even Methodists could steal bricks and mortar.

And what a building it was. In spite of the modest potential for enrollment, the university authorities decided to build
beyond their immediate needs. They brought in architect Fred-
eric W. Cumberland in the hope that he would design an eminent pile worthy of their lofty ambitions—and he did.
Cumberland decided that the new university building would be
constructed in the "collegiate gothic" style, a manner of architecture that unashamedly copied the medieval influence of truly
ancient university buildings such as those of Oxford and Cam-
bridge. But Cumberland soon ran into opposition and was

The Roundhouse (left): The colonnaded walkway, visible just to the right
of the Roundhouse, is where Reznikoff and Diabolos supposedly fought.
The gargoyles that each man reportedly carved are at the base of the small
chimney between the Roundhouse and the colonnade.

～

forced to entertain a number of gaudy alternatives, including ostentatious Italianate designs more at home on a palazzo than at a university just south of the Canadian Shield. Finally, having settled on a suitably vague "Norman" or "Early English" aesthetic, Cumberland went ahead and designed a building that left plenty of room for as much medieval ornamentation as could have been desired.

The foundations of University College were laid in 1856. When it came time to build the walls, bricks were used—more than a million—but not just any bricks. These had been fabricated locally by a newfangled machine method, a process that made their manufacture faster and cheaper, as opposed to being painstakingly shaped by manual labourers. Then, once these crisp, yellow bricks had been assembled into sturdy new walls, they were clad in stone to look aged. And that was how University College became emblematic of Canada itself—something essentially modern and new, but vested in the raiment of the past. To adorn the faux-ancient edifice, architect Cumberland brought in stone carvers from Europe, where such artisans were plentiful. The stonemasons would create gargoyles and accents to embellish the stodgy heft of the building's massive bulk.

So far, we have dealt in easily established facts, but the rest of the story relies upon the remarkable narrative of "John Smith," though he himself will not enter the story until some time later.

Two of the transplanted stonemasons were (according to Smith, as told to him by the ghost) Ivan Reznikoff and Paul Diabolos. Ivan Reznikoff was a large, powerful Russian Pole with swarthy features, dark, curly hair and a thick, black beard. His hands were hard and strong from years of working stone, his fingers thick and blunt, toughened by their daily toil. Reznikoff was very much of the Old World—he had endured long, drawn-out, hard labour and was a simple man with strong passions. For two years, he toiled away at the adornments of University College, chipping gargoyles out of lifeless stone and shaping the heavy stone pillars at the colonnaded entrance to the Roundhouse. He lived in a simple room at the Caer Howell Inn, where he fell in love. The object of his affections was the innkeeper's niece, Suzy, described as a beautiful girl, golden-haired, straight of figure and with rosy features. Suzy seemed to return the big stonemason's affections but not with the same ardour that Reznikoff offered them.

The second stonemason in our story is Paul Diabolos, a Greek from Corinth. Diabolos was fine featured and handsome, with dark, lustrous eyes. He had a quick temper and a sharp tongue. Diabolos had been trained as a sculptor in Italy and his native Greece. He was educated as well and spoke several languages. His stonework had the flare of inspiration, and he brought to life every figure he carved. Diabolos lived in a small room in the still-uncompleted college. He seems to very much represent the dawning of an age that was more preoccupied with style than substance.

In 1859, work on the building was wrapping up, and the college would soon be open. Day in, day out, in all weathers, fair or foul, Ivan Reznikoff had plied his trade with one hope in his heart—to save enough money so that he and Suzy could start a life together somewhere. Indeed, he had saved about $500, a considerable sum in those days, by giving Suzy most of his weekly wages to bank for him.

"When are you going to marry me?" asked Reznikoff, one summer evening as he and Suzy sat in the dining room at the Caer Howell Inn. "You put me off from day to day, from week to week, from month to month, and now the summer's almost gone."

"You know I promised that I'd marry you when your work was done," said Suzy. "Not before."

Reznikoff protested in vain that the work would be completed in just a few days. He entreated her to think of *their* new life together, reminded her that he had saved and sacrificed for *them*. He made it clear that he didn't care about anything as long as *she* was by *his* side. Suddenly overcome by a dark mood, he drew Suzy to him and growled a warning, "Don't play me false. I know you're a butterfly that wings its way from flower to flower, from tree to tree. I've watched your face until I know each fancy as it flits across your mind, and sometimes I see a look inside your eyes, when they fall upon that cursed Greek who daily works beside me, that sets my heart on fire, and makes me feel like taking him in my arms and crushing him to death.

Ivan Reznikoff, I presume? This gargoyle seems to be the obvious candidate for Diabolos' cruel caricature of his rival in love, Ivan Reznikoff—"more like a baboon than a man."

~

If I thought you cared a straw for him I'd twist his neck until his head fell off." At this juncture, Suzy's uncle came into the room; Reznikoff loosened his grip on Suzy and she slipped away.

The next day, Reznikoff was in a black mood when he met a fellow stonemason who told him in no uncertain terms that Suzy was indeed philandering in the arms of Paul Diabolos. Reznikoff did not want to believe it, but he knew in his heart that it was true. The other stonemason told Reznikoff that Suzy and Diabolos' trysting spot was a bench in front of the entrance to the Roundhouse. Of late, Diabolos and Reznikoff had been working side by side in that very spot, each chipping away at one of a pair of gargoyles tucked into the corner under the chimney. Reznikoff and his informant hatched a plot to hide in the shadows of the covered walkway that led to the stout oaken door. From there, they could eavesdrop upon the lovers.

That night, having hidden themselves in the shadows cast by the pillars of the walkway, Reznikoff and his companion watched as Diabolos and Suzy arrived and started canoodling on a nearby bench. It soon became apparent that the lovers had been making their own plans and that Suzy was not in love with Reznikoff but, rather, frightened of him.

"I wish that you would take me from this wretched town," Suzy sighed. "My heart grows weary, cooking, washing dishes, slopping round my uncle's inn. You promised me that you would go as soon as your work was done. I care not where I go so long as you are by my side."

In the shadows, Reznikoff's heart burned as he listened to Suzy ply Diabolos with the very blandishments that he himself had vainly pressed upon her only the day before. Now Diabolos suggested that the two of them might head west to start their new life together.

"'Tis a long way off," said Suzy. "It will cost a lot to take us there, even if we travel as the Indians do, with caravans and tents. My uncle told me all about it months ago."

"I have several hundred dollars in the bank," Diabolos reminded her, "and you said you had $500 there yourself." Suzy protested that the money she had belonged to Reznikoff. Diabolos brushed aside her argument, reasoning that Reznikoff would have simply drunk it away had she not been safeguarding it for him.

"But he told me yesterday that he would not let me play him false," said Suzy. "Sometimes I fear he'll do some evil deed, not to myself but to you. You know, he expects that I will marry him…"

"Marry you! Ha, ha! That old man!" sputtered Diabolos unkindly. "He's old enough to be your father. And ugly, he's more like a baboon than a man. Why, there's a gargoyle right behind us on the wall that I modelled on his hideous face. Ha, ha, ha!"

The two lovers then rose and giggled away into the night, but once they were out of earshot, Diabolos revealed to Suzy that he had detected Reznikoff lurking in the shadows and showed her the dagger he proposed to defend himself with if Reznikoff should threaten either of them. Suzy shivered and said she did not want blood spilled—anyone's.

The next day, Reznikoff and Diabolos worked side by side as they always did, chipping away at the stonework close to the entrance of the Roundhouse and its colonnaded walkway. Reznikoff was obviously drunk, and all day, Diabolos watched warily as the larger man chipped away at the adjacent gargoyle.

Diabolical visage? This is the gargoyle that Reznikoff may have carved to caricature his tormentor, Paul Diabolos—"how it grins and mocks."

~

When the sun went down and the rest of the workmen departed, Diabolos taunted Reznikoff, saying, "The pillars are unpolished and that gargoyle, there, shows all the hallmarks of a drunkard's touch. Look, besotted swine, how it grins and mocks!" With this, Reznikoff picked up the nearest weapon at hand, a hatchet left lying about after the day's work, and the fight was on.

Brandishing the hatchet, Reznikoff rushed into the walkway so quickly that Diabolos had no time to draw his dagger. Reznikoff grabbed him by the neck and swung the hatchet, but Diabolos twisted free and Reznikoff's blade glanced off the oaken planks of the door. Reznikoff swung the little axe several

Ghostly gashes? The gashes that Ivan Reznikoff's axe allegedly made in the door of the Croft Chapter House.

~

more times, each blow missing its mark and striking either the door or its iron hinges. Finally, Diabolos' back was against the door, and Reznikoff had him by the neck. Reznikoff raised the hatchet once more and drove it down with all the force he could muster. Diabolos, meanwhile, had reached around behind his back and managed to twist the handle of the door so that it opened inward. As the two men fell into the building, the axe split the edge of one of the door planks, leaving a massive gash just beside the handle. (As of 2012, when this account was written, the gash is still visible. Loudon also referenced it in 1928.)

The two combatants tumbled into the building, landing in a heap on the floor. Diabolos scrambled to his feet and ran off through the corridors with Reznikoff close behind. The pursuit ended, as do the best of them, with a frenzied chase up the stairs of a bell tower. Upon reaching the landing built for the bell ringer to stand upon, Diabolos noticed another short flight of stairs, quickly climbed them and then hid himself around a darkened corner. When Reznikoff staggered onto the landing, Diabolos sprang upon his adversary and stabbed him to death. He tipped the body down a well that had been dug beneath the tower steps, cleaned off his knife and ran off into the night. History relates no more of Paul Diabolos, nor of Suzy.

~

Sightings of Reznikoff's ghost seem to begin somewhere in the mid-1860s. According to W.J. Loudon, the ghost was most often seen "standing in the dusk of the twilight upon the gravel road, before the main doorway of the building: or, on moonlight nights, walking, with measured step, inside the little stone corridor hard by the Roundhouse."

In appearance, the apparition had, according to John Smith, "no legs or feet; no hands or arms; nothing but a vague and blurred appearance, a high crowned hat of some dark-coloured cloth, a mass of curly black hair and a black amorphous trunk." When Smith first encountered the ghost, it was talkative but mysterious, telling him that by day it slept in the college tower, only stirring its spectral limbs to come forth at night. After cryptically assuring Smith that it knew of death better than he, it disappeared and wasn't seen again by Smith until the end of his days at the university.

Next to see the ghost was undergraduate William Glenholme Falconbridge, later registrar of the university and after that an eminent judge. Falconbridge saw the figure in 1866, and his description closely tallied with W.J. Loudon's own account of spotting the figure two years later when he was just eight years old and with his grandmother: "All I was sure of was a shapeless form, a high-crowned conical hat, turned up behind and slanted in front, a mass of dark curly hair and a heavy beard of black." Loudon and his grandmother walked behind the ghost for several paces, but when they caught up to it near the Roundhouse, it simply melted away.

The spectre next appeared one night in 1892, when Robert McKim, the beadle of the college, was going about his chores in the bell tower. Suddenly, he saw what appeared to be a large, swarthy man with a beard and curly hair *slide down the bell rope and through an opening in the landing scarcely big enough for a cat.* Rushing down the stairs to the level below, the beadle was amazed to see the apparition floating in midair in front of a Latin inscription carved into the south wall, "mumbling foreign words and phrases that sounded like an invocation to some heathen god." When McKim shouted at the figure, it disappeared.

The final "documented" sighting of the ghost occurred in the late 1870s on John Smith's last night in his university digs.

In a reflective state of mind, thinking back over his university career and packing up his belongings, Smith polished off a bottle of his favourite whisky, Loch Katrine. He judiciously refrained from opening a second bottle, choosing instead to take a contemplative walk across the campus. Not long after, Smith once again met the thick-set, bearded figure he had first encountered as a freshman, but this time, the ghost was apparently fully materialized and had both feet and hands. Like a couple of old friends, the two of them headed up to Smith's room, where they smoked cigars and consumed the second bottle of Loch Katrine while the ghost of Reznikoff spun his tale of woe. In Smith's narrative, far from being a mysterious figure that disappears when approached, the ghost of Reznikoff is positively garrulous, regaling his host with a chatty account of his unhappy life and even unhappier death, then melting away with the morning light.

After a fire destroyed much of University College in 1890, a skeleton and a silver belt buckle were discovered at the bottom of the tower well. Loudon assumed the bones were those of Reznikoff and, aside from keeping the skull for himself, saw to it that they were respectfully buried beneath a maple tree in the Quadrangle, the exact location of the grave now lost to history. Once his bones were at rest, the ghost of Ivan Reznikoff walked no more, which would explain why no one has seen it for more than 100 years.

And what is left? There are gashes in the oaken door of the Roundhouse, an echo of the gash that Reznikoff felt in his heart when he learned that Suzy had given her love to another. Just a few feet away are two stone gargoyles, each allegedly carved by one of these rivals in love. The one on the left is the more grotesque, with angular, unnatural cheekbones and some sort of unspecified entrails caught in its teeth. Is this the one that Diabolos carved to ape Reznikoff's simian features? The gargoyle on the right is less horrific in appearance but has blunt, smug features, seemingly smiling with self-satisfaction. Is this Reznikoff's revenge? Is this the gargoyle Diabolos taunted him for? Visitors can judge for themselves.

It is fitting to close with John Smith's own recollection of the morning after Reznikoff's ghost had sat in his room to tell its tale of heartbreak:

...on the table, beside the lamp, stood an empty bottle, labelled Loch Katrine, and, beside it, lay a corkscrew and a cork. Circumstantial evidence perhaps but all I have to give. If you appeal to logic and to reason and put aside everything abnormal and bar all psychic phenomena from the evidence, then, of course, all you can infer from the story I have told you is what any judge and jury would undoubtedly decide, namely, there was a bottle of Highland whisky, labelled Lock Katrine, drunk in my room by some person or persons unknown.

Restless spirits, indeed.

Chapter Six

William Lyon Mackenzie King: The Prime Minister Who Spoke with the Dead

~

The August sun sets on a beautiful, wooded estate. The purple-blue light of approaching darkness rises up from the well-tended lawns and green, leafy glades. Rays from the sinking sun fall across stone ruins—ancient-looking gothic arches, curved stone walls with elaborately colonnaded windows and, set into a crumbling wall, a heraldic shield of carved stone showing three lions, the whole worn nearly smooth from years of exposure to the elements. There is an aura of serene mystery, and one can almost hear the echoes of chanting monks, knightly voices raised in good fellowship or perhaps even the distant ring of clashing swords. One would not be surprised to see Merlin the magician materialize in the pleasantly fading light. The scene described is not the ruins of Camelot, but rather the Québec estate formerly known as Kingsmere, the country getaway of William Lyon Mackenzie King, Canada's 10th and longest-serving prime minister.

Between 1921 and 1948, Mackenzie King spent 22 of those years as prime minister of Canada. He saw the nation through the ravages of the Great Depression and the horrors of World War II. A lifelong bachelor obsessed with the idea of pure, spiritual love, he was fixated on his mother. He named three of his four dogs "Pat." Although he lacked personal charisma, he spent so long in power thanks to his native intelligence, political acumen and a gift for appearing not to commit one way or the other. A devout Presbyterian who read the Bible every day of his adult life, he also regularly held séances and believed that he could speak to the souls of departed loved ones and titans from history.

There's something else you ought to know about William Lyon Mackenzie King before we dive into this particular chapter—he kept a diary and wrote nearly every day from 1893 to his death in 1950, a span of 57 years. Mackenzie King biographer C.P. Stacey called it "the most important single political document in twentieth-century Canadian history." It is from this remarkable account that we know so much about his private and public life.

Mackenzie King recounted his days in great detail, including personal idiosyncrasies (he was certain that whenever he looked at a clock and the hands were aligned, some deeper significance was evident) and descriptions of public events (elections, scandals and intrigues). He wrote candidly in the diary about his many communications with the spirits, but he kept his notes about séances and other sessions separately—they make equally fascinating reading.

Finally, it is worth remembering that the supposed ability to commune with the spirits of the dead—or "spiritualism" as it was called at that time—became a worldwide phenomenon in the wake of World War I. The war left millions upon millions of grieving parents, wives, siblings and children. The notion that one's loved ones might have not been horribly annihilated but, instead, may have simply "passed over" was obviously a comforting one. Self-proclaimed "mediums" could produce all sorts of strange phenomena—ghostly voices might speak through a gramophone trumpet, the medium could go into a trance and transcribe the words of the spirits via "automatic writing," a series of knocking sounds on the table could signify "yes" or "no" answers and even longer messages were communicated through "table rapping." Finally, the medium might simply speak the words of the spirits allegedly hovering around the table. Sir Arthur Conan Doyle, the creator of Sherlock Holmes, was a firm believer in spiritualism. However, Doyle's friend Harry Houdini, the famous escapologist and magician, famously offered $10,000 to any medium who could produce an effect that Houdini could not reproduce via the techniques and tradecraft of a professional illusionist. The reward was never claimed.

Mackenzie King was deeply committed to his family, though often oddly distant in his actual relationships with them. The one family member to whom he was never distant was his mother, Isabelle King. To say that Mackenzie King was a "mama's boy" is to grossly understate the depth and intensity of his devotion to her. When hunting for a wife, he would frequently compare potential mates to his mother in both the content of their characters and the strength of their religious convictions. After his mother's death, he wrote constantly that he felt her presence nearby, even going so far as to suspect that her spirit may have temporarily inhabited one of his three dogs named Pat. Consider, then, how deeply affected Mackenzie King must have been when, in rapid succession, one of his sisters, Bella, died in 1915, followed by his father in 1916, his mother in 1917 and, finally, his brother, Max, in 1922. The deaths of so many family members in so short a time, combined with his already strong religious faith, likely created in Mackenzie King a need that spiritualism could fill.

For a book of this sort, the relevance of Mackenzie King's spiritualist activities is simple—he attended séances all over the province, first at the Fulford mansion in Brockville, later at Laurier House, his Ottawa residence, and then at Doon, Kingston and a slew of others. For that matter, he also held "sittings," as he called them, not only across Canada, but also even when conducting official duties overseas, both during and after World War II. And with that, let us begin our roll call of both the places and spirits that figured in Mackenzie King's conversations from beyond the grave.

Kingswood, Mackenzie King's childhood home: If the child is the father of the man, then Kingswood arguably represents the birthplace of Mackenzie King's belief in the spirits. Certainly it was here that his odd relationship with his mother began.

~

March 1, 1925

This date marks the second time that Mackenzie King met Mrs. Rachel Bleaney, a local medium, while he was staying in Kingston on official business as prime minister. She had told his fortune four years earlier, but this session in 1925 appears to be the first time he was convinced that spirits from the other side were actually in attendance. Mrs. Bleaney was not a "direct voice" medium, but instead described to Mackenzie King the spirits she saw, as well as making predictions about the future.

In a five-page diary entry, Mackenzie King noted everything she had said, though his full conversion to a "believer" was probably delayed when many of Mrs. Bleaney's predictions turned out to be dead wrong. The quoted passages in the following paragraphs are taken directly from his diary.

According to Mackenzie King, Mrs. Bleaney "gave me a reading in the drawing room this afternoon, a truly remarkable experience….It was amazingly true of the past, & if true to the future will be astonishing beyond words, because so bold & daring in what it promised."

Among her predictions was that "There will be a general election soon. You will win that." In fact, Mackenzie King and his Liberal Party lost rather badly to Arthur Meighen's Conservatives, but he clung to power for another few months as the head of a minority government even though he had lost his own seat. The fallout from this defeat became known as the "King-Byng Affair" after Mackenzie King and Governor General Lord Byng disagreed on whether or not Mackenzie King could ask for the dissolution of Parliament (and so trigger another election) without first giving Meighen the chance to form a government. In the end, Meighen did briefly form a government but was soundly defeated by Mackenzie King's Liberals in the election that ensued when Meighen lost a confidence vote in the House.

Mrs. Bleaney also predicted the following:

You will marry, will marry a widow for the heart and spiritual nature….You may marry next year 1926 will be a very good year for you. (King never married and 1926 was a dreadful year for him, consumed as it was by the King-Byng Affair.)

You will live to be an old man [of] 78. (On another occasion, she said past 80, but Mackenzie King died when he was 75.)

You will not always live in Ottawa, indeed your work is but half over here. (In fact, King's career in Ottawa was, in some ways, just beginning—he would spend another 17 years as prime minister.)

February 26, 1932

This date marks a fairly typical session with one of Mackenzie King's favourite mediums, Mrs. Etta Wriedt of Detroit. A "direct voice" medium, Mrs. Wriedt channelled the words, if not the actual voices, of the dead, with the opinions and pronouncements of the deceased issuing directly from her lips. Mackenzie King is known to have attended sittings with Mrs. Wriedt at the Fulford mansion in Brockville, where he was introduced to her; Laurier House, his residence in Ottawa; Kingsmere, his retreat in Québec; and even her hometown of Detroit. According to King's notes, "Mrs. Wreidt [sic] arrived a few minutes after 11…I had 'conversations' with dear mother and Max, Senator Cox, Sir Wilfrid and grandfather." Here are some crib notes as to who these spirits had been during their corporeal lives:

"Dear mother" is Isabelle Mackenzie King (1843–1917). Mackenzie King had an infamously close relationship to his mother. Of all his lost loved ones, she was the soul he wished most urgently to communicate with. He constantly felt her presence after her death and spoke with "dear mother" at most of his séances. As we shall see later, she also figured frequently and prominently in Mackenzie King's "visions," which most of us would call dreams.

"Max" is Mackenzie King's brother (1878–1922). Noted as one of the few people able to speak honestly and critically to Mackenzie King, Dougall McDougall "Max" King died in Colorado at the age of 44. King had visited him just before he died, later writing that while holding his brother in his arms, he "told him I loved him with all my heart." King promised to look after Max's wife and family, as well as pay for Max's funeral expenses. He carefully itemized these expenses in his diary but then chided himself for thinking of money at such a grievous time of loss (Mackenzie King was already quite wealthy).

"Senator Cox" is George A. Cox (1840–1916). Not much is known of Mackenzie King's acquaintance with Cox, a wealthy Liberal senator, but it is worth noting that he usually seemed to favour posthumous communication with people whose advice he imagined he might value.

"Sir Wilfrid" is Sir Wilfrid Laurier (1841–1919). The seventh prime minister of Canada not only graces our five-dollar bill, but he was also a political mentor to Mackenzie King, who idolized Laurier and succeeded him as leader of the Liberal Party. Furthermore, Mackenzie King's Ottawa residence, Laurier House, was bequeathed to him by Sir Wilfrid's widow, Zoe, upon her death in 1921. Although it went to Mackenzie King because he was the leader of the Liberal Party, because of the wording of the will, the home became his personal property, much cherished and enjoyed after extensive renovations courtesy of a wealthy Liberal benefactor. In 1934, Mackenzie King, the leader of the Opposition to R.B. Bennett's Conservatives, sought Laurier's posthumous advice on which Canadians would be recommended for knighthoods. However, the long list of names that "Laurier" provided was completely wrong because no list of recommended knighthoods was even issued that year.

"Grandfather" is William Lyon Mackenzie (1795–1861). Mackenzie King was the maternal grandson of William Lyon Mackenzie, the first mayor of Toronto, a key instigator of the Upper Canada Rebellion of 1837, a political exile, a proponent of increased responsible government for Canada and an all-round agitator against the dreaded "Family Compact" of wealthy Protestants who owned or ran much of Ontario in the early 19th century.

Because of his grandfather's notable and tempestuous career, Mackenzie King felt that he had some kind of inherent destiny in public service and as a leader. He was also proud of his grandfather, though he never met him, and no doubt this shared ancestry with his beloved mother was just one more special bond that they had.

A short break here to look at one particular diary entry that, though no specific spirits are mentioned, illustrates the depth of Mackenzie King's belief in what he was experiencing. It also shines a brief but illuminating sidelight on his self-consciousness regarding his frequent communications with the dead (all underlined passages were so emphasized by Mackenzie King himself and appear this way in the diary).

June 30, 1932

Mrs. Wreidt [sic] came down....There can be <u>no doubt whatever</u> that the persons I have been talking with were the loved ones & others I have known and who have passed away. It <u>was the spirits of the departed</u>. There is no other way on earth of accounting for what we have all experienced this week. Just because it is so <u>self-evident</u> it seems hard to believe. It is like those who had Christ with them in His day, because it was all so simple, so natural, they would not believe and sought to destroy. I <u>know</u> whereof I speak that nothing but the presence [of] those who have

Homer Watson House: Today a museum and art gallery, Homer Watson House was the site of Mackenzie King's séance of April 13, 1934.

~

departed this life, but not this world, or vice versa could account for the week's experiences.

The 'conversations' in many cases have been so loud, so clear, etc. that I have felt great embarrassment at the servants in other parts of the house hearing what was said as I am sure they have.

April 13, 1934

As evidence of Mackenzie King's itinerant soothsaying, offered here is a short entry from his trip to Doon (now part of

Kitchener) to meet painter Homer Watson. Mackenzie King
was born in nearby Berlin (now also part of Kitchener). Beyond
this visit and shared stomping grounds, the connection between
Mackenzie King and Watson is unknown. However, from 1930
to 1935, Mackenzie King was leader of the Opposition and so
had much more time on his hands to pursue his spiritualist
beliefs. Some time in 1933, Mackenzie King was introduced to
"table rapping," a method of communication with the dead that
required no medium, but instead, two or more willing participants who could interpret knocking sounds ("rapping") that
were supposedly actuated by spirits upon a small table that was
placed between the living participants. It was probably this
method that Mackenzie King used on his visit to Homer Watson when he wrote in his diary, "tried the table with Watson and
got some splendid results." The "splendid results" were likely the
table's prediction that Mackenzie King would win the upcoming election (which he did).

November 25, 1934

Still languishing in the Opposition and seemingly with
abundant time on his hands, Mackenzie King wrote this entry
in his diary:

*After Church spent til about 11 with the little table, get-
ting the most amazing results as will be seen from what
follows. I came home feeling, that there could be no question of the truth of what had been revealed—that I had*

been talking with Leonardo Da Vinci—Lorenzo di Medicii [sic] *& Pasteur. As well as father & Max…the presence of the others makes clear how we move into the circles where like attracts like in the other world more than here.*

It is interesting to note that Mackenzie King, no longer prime minister and now in the Opposition, seems to readily identify his father (a small-time lawyer thwarted from running for political office by his domineering wife), his brother (a sickly doctor who died young) and, by extension, himself, with three giants of history:

Leonardo da Vinci (1452–1519). Regarded as the archetypical "Renaissance Man," da Vinci's most famous work is probably his painting, The Mona Lisa, but his long list of artistic and scientific pursuits includes sculpting, music, architecture, anatomy, geology and botany, among others. It is not clear from available accounts what da Vinci and Mackenzie King discussed during this sitting.

Lorenzo de' Medici (1449–92). This Florentine statesman was a wealthy diplomat, politician and scholar. In essence, he ruled the Florentine republic, and when he died, the alliance of Italian states over which he had presided collapsed.

Louis Pasteur (1822–95). The French chemist and microbiologist was a titan of modern science, inventing the first vaccines for rabies and anthrax, as well as developing the process named after him, pasteurization, that prevents beer, wine and milk from spoiling. He also helped prove that germs cause illness. Interestingly, after the séance cited above, Pasteur considerately "returned" two days later on November 27 to make a prognosis for Mackenzie King's dog, Pat, who was feeling under the weather.

Observers noted that whenever Mackenzie King consulted the spirits, their responses tended to confirm his pre-existing opinions. In most cases, they advised him to be cautious, as was his nature, anyway. For instance, after World War II, Mackenzie King sought the advice of recently deceased U.S. president Franklin Delano Roosevelt regarding the defection of Soviet cipher clerk Igor Gouzenko—the incident that would spark the beginning of the Cold War. The spirit of FDR advised him to be careful.

Mackenzie King does not appear to have followed any specific spirit's advice and, for that matter, the spirits never really offered any. It is a relief, then, that his essentially sober, sensible outlook was the one that informed his decisions as prime minister. When he made mistakes, they were because of misjudgements concerning this earthly realm and not undue obeisance to the next. Although Mackenzie King frequently mentioned his sittings in his diary, more detailed notes of each session were kept separately, as is the case with the account that follows. The tendency of the spirits to confirm Mackenzie King's existing opinions is quite evident in the transcription, with a veritable *Who's Who* of the afterlife chiming in to confirm that Mackenzie King was *destined* to lead Canada.

Here are crib notes for spirits not already known to us:

"King (father)" is John King (1843–1916). Mackenzie King's father was a lawyer who struggled to support his family and was forbidden by his wife, Isabelle, from running for public office, which he desperately wanted to do. Mackenzie King respected his father and, as an adult, gave him considerable financial assistance, though the son rarely let the father forget this and, at times, fils even chastised père for not being more successful.

"Gladstone, Mr. Wm." is William Ewart Gladstone (1809–98). Prime minister of Britain on four separate occasions, Gladstone racked up a total of 16 years in office. Mackenzie King likely revered him.

"Lord Morley" is John Morley, 1st Viscount of Blackburn (1838–1923). This British statesman got his start in life as a reporter and later became a newspaper editor. It seems likely that Mackenzie King admired his liberal values and perhaps saw a connection between Morley's journalism career and that of his own grandfather. Over the course of his tempestuous life, William Lyon Mackenzie published several newspapers that espoused his own political views.

"Lord Oxford" is H.H. Asquith, 1st Earl of Oxford and Asquith (1852–1928). Mackenzie King seems to have had a weakness for Liberal prime ministers of the UK (or perhaps their deceased spirits had a weakness for him). Known as Lord Oxford after his ascendancy to the peerage, during his time as premier, Asquith instituted several social reforms that would have appealed to Mackenzie King.

"Lord Grey" is Edward Grey, 1st Viscount Grey of Fallodon (1862–1933). Yet another British Liberal, Fallodon also served as Foreign Secretary and later became leader of the Liberal Party in the House of Lords. He may or may not have uttered the words attributed to him upon the outbreak of World War I, "The lamps are going out all over Europe. We shall not see them lit again in our time."

"Alexander Mackenzie" (1822–92) was Canada's second prime minister. He was no relation to Mackenzie King.

"St. Luke" is a biblical figure, the apostle and author of the New Testament's Gospel of Luke.

"St. John" is another biblical figure, probably John the Evangelist.

"Joan" is Joan Patteson, perhaps Mackenzie King's only true friend. A married woman, she was his confidante, a constant source of support and a fellow believer in spiritualism who frequently participated in table rapping sessions with him.

And with this lengthy cast of characters complete, now for the séance! The following passage is taken directly from Mackenzie King's diaries:

> *Laurier House, Ottawa, Oct. 6, 1935*
> *King (father)*
> > *Love from all here to Joan and you*
> > *I love to speak to you again.*
> > *Laurier is here.*
> *Laurier (Sir Wilfrid)*
> > *Love from Lady Laurier & me to Mr. & Mrs. Patteson*
> > *and you.*
> > *Long ago God meant that I should tell you that*
> > *you should be Prime Minister again.*
> > *Let Gladstone speak.*
> *Gladstone, Mr. Wm.*
> > *K—so good of Mr. G to come.*
> > *I love to come.*
> > *Look out for long reign as Prime Minister.*
> > *God meant that I should tell you that.*
> > *Let Morley speak.*
> *Lord Morley*
> > *Long ago God meant that Gladstone would tell*
> > *you that you would be prime minister for a long time.*
> > *Let Asquith speak.*

Lord Oxford

> *Long ago I said that Canada would show other*
> *parts of the Empire the way.*
> *Long ago God meant that you should lead the*
> *British Empire in the way it should go.*
> *God meant that you should be Prime Minister*
> *for that purpose.*
> *Let Grey speak.*

Lord Grey

> *Long ago God meant that you should know the*
> *way to peace. Let Mackenzie speak.*

[There follows a garbled exchange while the sitters
determine that "Mackenzie" is, in this case, not William
Lyon Mackenzie, but rather Alexander Mackenzie,
second prime minister of Canada.]

Mackenzie, Alex

> *Long ago God meant that another Mackenzie*
> *should be Prime Minister of Canada.*
> *Let your grandfather speak.*

Mackenzie, W.L.

> *Love to Mrs. Patteson & you from mother and me.*
> *God meant that you should take up my work again.*
> *Long ago God meant that I should try to make*
> *his will prevail on earth as it is in heaven.*
> *I tried to do my best. Long ago I tried to serve his*
> *holy will. Long ago I suffered greatly for him.*

He will repay me through you.

Let St. Luke speak.

St. Luke

Love to Mrs. Patteson and you.

Long ago I wanted to help you.

More power will be given to you from God.

Let St. John speak.

St. John

Love to Mrs. Patteson and you.

Long ago I wanted to tell you that God had
chosen you to show men & nations how they
should live. Let your mother speak.

Mother

Love to Joan & Godfroy [Joan's husband] & you from
all of us

Joan said something about the meaning of "Long ago"—
[mother could] Long ago means that we were in a for-
mer state

"Long ago" means we are higher up in heaven.

"Long ago" means that we are happy here in God's
service.

Let father speak.

Father

Long ago I told Nelson that you would have a
high place in the affairs of Canada.

Long ago I knew that God meant you would be

Prime Minister.

Long ago I was told that you would honour my name

Long ago your mother dreamt that you would

be Prime Minister.

Let Mother speak.

Mother

Long ago I dreamt that you would succeed Sir Wilfrid

Laurier.

Long ago I knew that God meant you to be Prime

Minister.

Long ago I [more than] knew that God meant

that you would serve his holy will.

Good night.

Have you ever read such a self-aggrandizing load of rubbish? It is revealing that none of the spirits told Mackenzie King to stop being so insecure and get on with the job of governing. For this writer, the true mysteries of William Lyon Mackenzie King are human, many and manifold—how could a person, in many ways so out of touch with the realities of everyday life, still have broad enough electoral appeal to be prime minister for 22 years? This strange dichotomy is perhaps best illustrated by an incident that occurred at the height of the Great Depression. Mackenzie King, by then quite wealthy, halted his grandiose plans to install more stone ruins at his Kingsmere estate when he realized the potentially disastrous optics of spending so much money on something so frivolous when so many had so little. Even at the height of his pseudo-mystical quest, Mackenzie

King had the good sense to realize how the average person would perceive his actions.

Also heartbreaking, but probably not surprising, is Mackenzie King's inability to balance his publicly compassionate persona with a private side that was often stingy, with both time and money. For example, he couldn't find the few seconds necessary to mail a birthday cheque for $100 to his nephew, but then he later felt bad for spending so much money on "old furniture" when there was a "young life" in need of sustenance. Like so many of us, he often seemed saddened when he realized something's importance only in retrospect.

Finally, and perhaps most sadly, was Mackenzie King's lifelong but unfulfilled quest to find a true soulmate, a helpmeet to support him in his struggles, both in this world and the next. For his entire life, the chance to be in love was something that King spent a great deal of time and energy actively seeking. In the end, though, his many eccentricities and oddly skewed core personality traits—in many ways, the very things that made him such an able politician, admired by so many—were also the coffin nails that ended any opportunity he might have ever had to meet a woman who could be his life partner. For, in the end, although William Lyon Mackenzie King never expressed anything but overall satisfaction with his political career and his place in history, to an outside observer, his life seems bounded in many ways by self-absorption and, most tragically, loneliness.

Chapter Seven

The Girl Who Had Lived Before

~

O
ne day, during the summer of 1966, if you happened to be hovering over the little community of Bala- clava on the shores of Georgian Bay, you might have observed the following: a middle-aged man and a young woman with bright red hair, both running for their lives from a charg- ing bull. With no other escape route, they scrambled for a fence that separated the bull's field from the Meaford tank range, a large plot of abandoned land used for target practice by the Canadian military. Knowing it was an off-day for the tank range, the two hurried to escape the stamping, snorting beast close on their heels.

As the young woman threw one leg over the fence rail, she turned to the man and said, "They ought to call this place Bullaclava."

"Very funny," said the man and clambered over after her.

The young woman was 17-year-old Joanne MacIver, a resident of nearby Orillia. The middle-aged man was writer Jess Stearn, who had come all the way from New York to search

for evidence that Joanne had lived a previous life as Susan Ganier, a farm wife in rural Ontario who was born in 1835 and died
in 1903. In one sense, then, this story starts in the 1830s. But in
a more immediate sense, for readers who are rightly wondering
why an investigation into reincarnation should require two people to escape from a charging bull by jumping over a fence into
a tank range, the story begins one evening in October 1962.

On the night in question, it was after supper in the
MacIver household. The family, Joanne's parents and various
siblings, were scattered throughout the house. Two friends of
Joanne's, Barbara White and Paul Torrance, had unexpectedly
dropped by, and the three of them were playing cards. The conversation turned to hypnosis. Paul was adamant that no one
could hypnotize him. As it happened, Joanne's father, Ken
MacIver, was an amateur hypnotist, having "put people under"
for entertainment when he was in the air force. Joanne sum-
moned her father and asked if he would try to hypnotize the
skeptical Paul Torrance. Mr. MacIver tried, but true to his word,
Torrance was not susceptible. However, upon looking up at his
daughter, MacIver saw that her eyes were closed and that she
had gone where young Torrance could (or would) not—into
a hypnotic trance.

Upon trying to regress his daughter to past events in her
current life, Ken MacIver stumbled upon not one but several
past lives that his daughter recalled—she had been a male called
Michael, seemingly in pre-revolutionary France, an African

woman named Oi who lived in a bamboo hut, a settler named Suzette in Québec and a fugitive slave in early 18th-century Virginia. But the "core" past life, the most recent and the one that seemed to have been most fully lived, was that of Susan Ganier (pronounced *Ga-nyay*), born in 1835 to a family of French Canadian extraction near the little community of Massie, near present-day Owen Sound.

From this first accidental session and several more formal ones that followed, some led by Ken MacIver and others by professional hypnotists, a remarkably vivid picture of Susan Ganier's life emerged. As a little girl, she had been known as "Suzy." Her parents, Mason and Catherine, ran a modest general farm, growing crops and keeping livestock. Life was a hardscrabble existence in early rural Ontario, with few luxuries or even points of interest. The family sometimes attended a nearby Methodist church, but Suzy recalled that none of them had clothes they felt were nice enough in which to worship. She desultorily attended school but dropped out when winter and a lack of warm clothes made the journey too difficult. During the warm months, she and her brother, Reuben, sometimes played in the fields along with Tommy Marrow, the young son of a neighbouring farmer. Once, she remembered, they got into trouble for knocking over cornstalks during a drought. She also remembered rowing in Georgian Bay near a location called Vail's Point.

For the most part, the children's days involved doing chores to help out around the farm. One of Suzy's jobs was to clean out the barn once a week. She remembered that it contained about eight cows with some pigs over in the corner; according to her, they made quite a mess. Reuben's job was to help his father with the plow, a chore that Suzy would have much preferred to do. The farm's orchard produced apples, so pies were abundant. Supper items might include bread, pickles or cucumbers and milk from the farm's cows. Suzy vividly recounted her horror at watching her father slaughter a pig that the family later ate.

Certain turns of phrases uttered by Joanne/Suzy are difficult to imagine as having been picked up by a high school student in 1960s Orillia. For example, when Suzy and her father travelled into Massie, they went not by "horse and buggy," but rather by "the buggy and horses." Later, when Suzy had grown into Susan and was a young woman eager to marry, she recalled that her father had said she was like "the foal who was ready to ride," another expression that it seems unlikely for Joanne to have consciously heard before.

Although interjected with sadness and disappointment, the next chapter of Susan's life was considerably more vivid and happy than her rather dull childhood. This began at the age of 17, when she married her childhood playmate, Tommy, aged 21, and became Susan Marrow. A pragmatic young woman, she confessed that although she loved Tommy, she didn't want to get married until he had gotten his own farm. The young couple was wed by a travelling lay preacher named McEachern at a location Susan referred to simply as "the Twin Churches." Watching the hypnotized Joanne MacIver remember Susan's newly married life, writer Jess Stearn recounted that her voice rang with joy as she said, "Here he comes, he's coming in from the barn and I'm on the porch. Oh, he picked me up and swung me around. Oh, I am so happy, I am so happy. Tommy says he's happy, too. That's why he swung me around."

Tragedy soon followed, though. Susan's mother, Catherine, passed away in her sleep and was discovered on the couch by Mason. Then her brother, Reuben, married a woman named Rachel, to whom Susan took a distinct dislike. But for the most part, times were happy as Tommy and Susan Marrow built a life for themselves on their own farm in Sydenham Township, not far from the St. Vincent Line, near present-day Meaford. It was only a few miles from her parents' farm. Susan set about fixing up the couple's small, white farmhouse, putting in a walkway to bridge the little creek that flowed in front of it and installing a small porch at the front door. There she would busy herself about her chores and wait tranquilly on the porch when it was time for Tommy to come in from the fields.

Susan shared other details of daily rural life, too. The general store in Massie was called either MacGregor's or Milligan's, or had perhaps been jointly run by two proprietors with these names—Susan was hazy on this. The nearest neighbour was named Hilda Black, but Susan did not know her particularly well and seemed loath to engage with her because Hilda was "poor." Other families that Susan saw socially were the O'Learys, the Browns and the Speedies. Mrs. Margaret Speedie ran the post office in nearby Anaan, about two miles from the Marrows. She and Susan were particularly good friends and sometimes attended bakes and quilting bees together.

Under hypnosis, Joanne/Susan recalled two blights upon this tranquil life. The first was an individual named Yancey. He was a labourer who lived nearby and occasionally helped Tommy around the Marrow farm. During early hypnosis sessions, Susan would mention him but refused to be drawn out as to why she didn't like him. Finally, it emerged that Yancey had made unwelcome advances to her one summer day when the two of them were alone in the kitchen. The lascivious Yancey had encircled her waist with his arms and pulled her toward him. In protest, she hit and kicked him, scurrying over to the stove and picking up a shovel to protect herself. At this point, Yancey appears to have sensibly bolted, and Susan ran out to the field where Tommy was cutting grass. Her husband was, of course, angry and threatened to give Yancey a beating if the farmhand ever came back, which he never did.

The other, more significant and lasting blot on the Marrows' happiness was the fact that Susan could not bear children. Although she understood and enjoyed sex, Susan was greatly disappointed that she could not conceive, sadly saying,

"We couldn't make them yet." Later, two French speakers who were observing this particular hypnosis session pointed out that this appeared to be an English translation of an idiomatic French phrase, further lending credence to Mason Ganier's alleged French heritage. It emerged that, sadly, all the many little improvements and touches Susan had added to the Marrow home were projects she had given herself to fill the void she felt as a childless married woman.

Despite its central disappointment—the inability to bear children—this middle period of Susan Marrow's life was definitely the happiest. Her descent into old age, loneliness and death was particularly grim, starting with Tommy's death in 1863.

Tommy was working in the barn when his shoulder and neck were accidentally punctured by the curved blade of a scythe, and Susan's beloved husband bled to death in her arms. After this, Susan's grief only deepened when her father died as well. She never remarried, nor did she go to live with Reuben's family, since she still did not like Rachel, his wife. Instead, she sold the farm and went to live in an abandoned shack on someone else's land a couple of kilometres down the road from her farm. She simply asked the owner if she could live in it, and he said yes.

Here, her life shifted into a solitary cycle of daily chores and very little socialization. In the summer, she looked after the garden. As winter approached, she brought in the vegetables and covered the garden with manure. She split her own wood, though a neighbour called Mr. Thompson sometimes helped. She acquired three cats and lived a life of poverty, alone in her little shack.

Susan described herself at age 34 as "Sort of heavy. My hair is brown, faded, now in a bun at the back." She wore a long skirt down to her ankles and a rather shapeless blouse on top. By the time Susan was 42, she felt old and fat. At 48, she had arthritic legs. The most remarkable thing about this phase in Susan Marrow's life was the physical change it brought about in young Joanne MacIver. Numerous witnesses, including her parents and Jess Stearn, the rather skeptical New York writer, observed that as Susan Marrow aged, Joanne MacIver's face physically changed—the muscles sagged and her voice became thin and reedy. During other hypnosis sessions, especially if she was reliving the period after Tommy's death, her eyes seemed to slant, narrowing in grief and making her look as though she was of Asian extraction. During one early session, not only did her eyes slant, but the very structure of her cheeks and face also seemed to change. Everyone who witnessed these remarkable alterations felt that the changes could not have been produced by some sort of "act" on Joanne's part—she was clearly living these experiences, whether they had happened or not.

The entire latter half of Susan's life was one of solitude and poverty as she eked out her days in the small shack. She occasionally received letters from friends or from Reuben, but for the most part, Susan seems to have had little social interaction. She began to have ghostly visitations from her father, who would come and sit in a nearby chair, listening and speaking to her. Occasionally, she offered him tea, forgetting that he could not drink it. Among her few earthly friends was a frequently drunk man named MacGregor, who had also been a friend of Tommy's. MacGregor could bring a smile to the widow's face as he related funny stories of his drunken exploits. Once he told Susan that he had been blearily staggering home one night when he found himself confronted by a bear. Panicking, MacGregor climbed a tree and stayed up it all night, only to discover that with the return of morning (and some semblance of sobriety), the fearsome bear was nothing more ferocious than a cow.

Finally, during the harsh winter of 1903, Susan died, simply saying that she was "tired and cold." Her restless spirit lost awareness of itself for a few months until she returned for own funeral, not held until the spring when the ground was soft enough for digging. And with that, the sometimes joyful, often wretched life of Susan Ganier came to an end. Our story, however, is really just beginning. After all, there's still that matter of the charging bull to explain.

~

Jess Stearn was in his mid-fifties in 1966 and already a well-established writer. His early books, all nonfiction, had focused on then-marginalized people in society—drug addicts, prostitutes, gays and lesbians. By the mid-1960s, though, his interests were drifting toward reincarnation and the paranormal. In 1965, he had published a book entitled, *Yoga, Youth and Reincarnation*.

But for all that, Stearn was skeptical about Joanne MacIver's claims. He didn't doubt that she was genuinely experiencing the events she described during hypnosis—she obviously really "meant" and believed what she was recounting. In fact, as he delved further into researching the book that he would rather pointlessly call *The Search for the Girl with the Blue Eyes*, Stearn found Joanne somewhat reluctant to dwell on her past life. An earlier newspaper article about her in the *Toronto Star* had brought largely unwelcome attention. Her appearance on a TV program with writer and broadcaster Pierre Berton was even worse because Berton, who plainly believed none of it, was condescending and faintly mocking. At 17, Joanne was simply eager to get on with living the life that was currently hers— she only consented to the hypnosis sessions that would form the basis of Stearn's book at his urging.

Like Fox Mulder in the TV series *The X-Files*, Jess Stearn wanted to believe, but he needed some sort of evidence that a woman named Susan Ganier had lived at the times and places mentioned during Joanne MacIver's past-life regressions. He had his work cut out for him. Rural 19th-century Ontario was neither a time nor a place where writing things down was a priority—members of the labouring class were often barely, if at all, literate. And, of course, there were no computers, social insurance numbers, healthcare cards or drivers' licences, nor much of anything in the way of standardized bureaucratic record keeping—in Ontario, even provincial death records were not kept until 1879.

But for all that, there were some leads. Journalist Allen Spraggett's article about Joanne, entitled "Has this little girl lived twice?" that appeared in the *Toronto Star* on February 6, 1965, rather amazingly confirmed some key details, and these made an obvious starting point for Jess Stearn. There had, in fact, been a village named Massie in Holland Township near Owen Sound, though it had long since devolved from a settlement into a mere crossroads. The name "Massie" was only known to a few rather elderly locals. Vail's Point was also a real place, described as "the apex of a promontory which juts out into Georgian Bay between Owen Sound and Meaford." It was from clues such as these that the probable locations of the Ganier and Marrow farms were established as likely being in the area now taken up by the Meaford tank range.

But there was more—the name of Susan Marrow's friend, Margaret Speedie, appeared on a headstone beside that of her husband in the nearby cemetery at Anaan:

In Memory of William Speedie
Died March 1, 1885, Aged 79
A native of Perthshire, Scotland
and
Also his wife, Margaret Eadie

Died June 27, 1909, Aged 86 Years
A native of Perthshire, Scotland

This was really something—there had been a Margaret Speedie, and she would have lived at roughly the same time and in the right area to have known Susan Ganier. But all was not quite as it seemed—when Stearn consulted *Smith's Gazeteer* for 1888, he discovered that at that time, Margaret Speedie was listed as the proprietor of a general store, presumably having taken over after the death of her husband. The postmaster was called Milligan, a name Susan had recalled as belonging to a shopkeeper. There was also a listing for a blacksmith named MacGregor, but he was in business for himself and not the joint proprietor of an establishment with Milligan, as Susan had remembered. Prior to her marriage, when she was a little girl, Susan had recalled that the mill where her father took his oats to be ground was run by a man named McKelver, but the flour mill in 1888 was run by a man named Brown, though this would have been nearly 40 years after the girlhood of Susan Ganier, so a change of owners was not out of the question. All in all, not bad for a fugitive spirit trapped in the body of a young girl.

Unfortunately, the most likely witness to corroborate the existence of Susan Marrow was dead—not Susan herself, but a recently deceased elderly farmer named Arthur Eagles. Joanne MacIver's father, Ken, had come across Eagles during his own search for some proof of Susan Marrow's existence. Before Eagles' death, he had been hale, hearty and lucid for all of his 85 years. Furthermore, Stearn discovered that Eagles' sharp mind and good memory were held in high regard by those who knew him and even those who did not particularly like him. Upon being asked about the reliability of any affidavit Eagles might have signed, one local said, "I'd close my eyes and sign it after him…" Stearn also met Paul Uhlig, an acquaintance of the MacIvers who had accompanied Ken to his interview with Arthur Eagles and swore that the questions had not been leading, and that much of the startling information had first been mentioned by Eagles himself.

Eagles' affidavit began, "I knew Susan Marrow when I was between the ages of fourteen and twenty-one years of age." Uhlig swore that, although Ken had asked Eagles whether he knew any Ganiers, it had been Eagles who first mentioned the "Widow Marrow," using Susan's married name. "Her husband Tommy," Eagles' deposition continued, "died about the time I was three years old, from what my parents told me. The Ganiers were friends of Jack Stitt, an acquaintance of mine. I often saw them in his company and believe they farmed near Strathavon—in Sydenam Township, Grey County."

In statements not included in the affidavit, Eagles said he remembered a person named Yancey living in the area and also recalled a mill owner named McKelver and that his mill had been "in back" of the Twin Churches (where Susan Marrow said she had been married), now in the Meaford tank range. In his sworn statement, Arthur Eagles described what Susan Marrow had looked like in the latter years of her life:

> *Susan Marrow was average height, around five feet, four inches* [162.5 centimetres] *tall and was well built, and really an average good-looking woman with a weight of around one hundred and fifty pounds* [68 kilograms] *when she was around sixty years of age. I do not believe that she was much older than sixty when she died.*

Sharp-eyed readers will note that a death at the age of 60 in 1903 would make Susan Marrow about 30 years *younger* than she herself recalled.

Next, Stearn decided to seek permission to enter the Meaford tank range, where both the Ganier and Marrow farms were supposed to have been located. After securing the necessary clearance from Major Malone, the official in charge, Stearn made a series of visits to the area in and around the tank range, sometimes with Ken MacIver, Joanne and others in tow, other times with just Joanne. Before these visits, neither Joanne nor her father had ever had access to the tank range.

The findings were inconclusive, partly because of the years of bombardment that any surviving structures had endured as the practice targets of artillery shells. To be sure, the visitors discovered ruins in locations that Joanne recognized from her previous life's memories, but the buildings had been blasted down to the ground and any sort of identification was nearly impossible. In one instance, amazingly, Joanne pointed toward a rather undistinguished-looking patch of soil and said that a well had been there—upon scraping away a layer of refuse, Stearn and Major Malone did discover an ancient, disused well. On their second visit, after they were chased over the fence by the bull, Joanne and Stearn discovered a small, single-room building in the location Joanne said had been the site of the Twin Churches; there, they also discovered a fragment of a gravestone with some inconclusive markings on it. Joanne led the way to the ruins of a building that she identified as her and Tommy's farmhouse, but, though she became very emotional here, the layout was rather different than what she remembered. They were unable to find any trace of Tommy's grave nearby, where Susan Marrow had chosen to have him buried.

But the search for proof that either the Ganier or Marrow families had ever existed was considerably less fruitful. Returning from their final trip to the tank range, Stearn and Joanne visited an elderly widow who, though she could recall neither the Ganiers nor the Marrows, did remember the Twin Churches and calmly said they had been Methodist and Baptist. Archival sources—diaries, newspapers, military records and other documents—proved equally frustrating. A cover-to-cover reading of the diary of Peter Fuller, a Meaford bank manager who had died in 1890, mentioned neither the Ganiers nor the Marrows, but then again, they were not families likely to be known or written about by one of the town worthies. A monument to Meaford's dead in World War I listed neither Ganiers nor Marrows. Local voters' lists prior to 1909 were no longer extant. Stearn continued his search at the Ontario Archives in Toronto as well, even hiring a researcher to carry on after he returned to New York, but no mention of either Ganiers or Marrows, or even names that were phonetically similar, was discovered.

And what of Joanne MacIver? When Jess Stearn met her in the 1960s, she was a beautiful young woman who seemed to have wisdom and knowledge beyond her years. At the same time, she was grounded and far more eager to live life in the present than to dwell in the past. According to Stearn, the shared life of Susan Marrow had made Joanne MacIver very eager to marry and have children, possibly even more so than many other young women of her age and era. He was constantly struck by how energetic and forward-looking she was for someone who had lived before—in other words, she was a perfectly normal teenager for her time. While she seemed to acknowledge and accept the life of Susan Marrow into the memories and experiences of her own life, they didn't especially preoccupy her, and throughout the period when Stearn was researching the book, she remained far more interested in her day-to-day life and prospects for the future, only consenting to additional hypnosis sessions at Stearn's urging and because she felt it might please her father. For someone who had experienced the sobering, often trying life of an early Ontario settler, Joanne herself remained positive, energetic and young.

I was fortunate enough to contact Joanne MacIver prior to the writing of this book. Now, as then, she comes across as grounded, approachable and positive. She very civilly declined to be interviewed.

Chapter Eight

A Haunting in the Suburbs

In the spring of 1968, Canadian newspapers were full of politics. South of the border, Bobby Kennedy, younger brother of the late president, was campaigning hard in the primaries, little knowing that on June 6, he would be killed by an assassin's bullets. In Canada, Pierre Trudeau was preparing to fight his first election since he had become leader of the Liberal Party and, by default, prime minister of Canada. On June 25, voters would send him into office with a healthy majority, riding the crest of "Trudeaumania."

But in May 1968, all these events still lay in the future, and in the West Toronto suburb of Etobicoke, all eyes were on an old farmhouse on Prince Edward Drive. Spurred by a series of articles in the *Toronto Telegram*, crowds of rowdy sightseers and thrill-seekers descended upon the house, shouting, throwing things and trying to break in. Like any major paper, the *Telegram* covered national and world events, but at that moment, it was a story of local—and possibly supernatural—interest that had captured readers' imaginations.

The house was haunted.

~

The old house on Prince Edward Drive had been built around 1890, give or take a couple of years. Various generations of the same family lived in it for the next several decades, and in 1941, William Tomlinson, the great-grandson of the original builder, converted it into a duplex with two separate apartments aboveground and a basement suite below. At some point, the house was sold as a rental property to the Szostak family, who were the landlords in 1968.

In May 1968, the tenants included English teacher Archie Nishimura, who lived in the basement apartment, as well as Mr. and Mrs. Albert Cracknell, who lived on the ground floor with their youngest daughter, 10-year-old Shirley. The Cracknells had rented their apartment for 11 years. In the second-storey, two-bedroom apartment lived the Cracknells' 27-year-old daughter, Carol Hawkins, and her husband, Roy Hawkins, who was a year older than his wife. The Hawkins had three children, Trudy and Sherry, four and five years old, respectively, with nine-month-old Steven rounding out the busy young household. The attic immediately above the Hawkins' apartment was not occupied—at least not by any earthly agency.

The Hawkins family was in the midst of two different stressful situations. Steven, the baby boy, had a severe ear and mastoid infection, and doctors had told the Hawkins that unless both his ears were operated upon, their son's life was in danger. However, the operation carried a significant chance of deafness. As if this weren't enough, Roy Hawkins worked at the Goodyear Tire and Rubber Company, where the entire workforce was shortly expected to go on strike, meaning that the burgeoning family's sole source of income would vanish just as they needed it most. Unfortunately, the Hawkins were about to experience a third kind of stress that nothing could have prepared them for.

The trouble started the night of Monday, April 29. That evening, Carol and Roy were lying in bed. By about 12:30 AM, Roy had fallen asleep, but Carol was still awake, lying in bed next to her husband. Then she heard slow, deliberate footsteps, followed by what was described as "screeching laughter." Terrified, Carol woke Roy.

"It sounded like a middle-aged woman," Carol said. "I'd swear to God it was right in the room." Amazingly, Carol and Roy lay there listening to this spine-chilling clamour for what they later estimated to have been about 20 minutes (though it could easily have been 20 seconds that *felt* like 20 minutes). At some point, they realized that Sherry and Trudy might also be hearing the sounds and could be frightened. When Carol and Roy got up, the sounds immediately stopped. Upon entering their daughters' bedroom, the terrified but now relieved parents found the children sleeping peacefully. Roy went downstairs to his in-laws' apartment and woke them, only to discover that they had heard nothing. Roy went back upstairs, and he and his wife tremulously went back to bed. But a few hours later, as Carol was lying half asleep in their bed, she experienced the sensation of someone standing over her. Opening her eyes, she saw no one but suddenly felt an extreme chill pass through her body, later saying, "It felt like something had walked right through me."

"We went up there the next day and searched from one end to the other," Roy later said. Indeed, that morning, Roy and his father-in-law, Albert Cracknell, climbed the stairs to the attic and hunted for clues. Albert was sure that some sort of animal had caused the disturbance. The nearby Parklawn Cemetery was known to be infested by raccoons; perhaps one of them had gotten into the house. Alas, the two men's search revealed neither any traces of an animal, nor any way an animal might have entered the house through the attic.

The next night, the frightened couple could not sleep and, to their horror, at about 2:00 AM, the sounds of walking began again, as though someone was deliberately and unhurriedly pacing circles up in the attic. The sounds would cease for a few minutes, then start again, stop again and then start once more. The spectral footsteps went on like this, stopping and starting, until the windows grew grey with daylight, whereupon the ghostly footsteps ceased.

On Wednesday, Roy and Carol drove to the sprawling Toronto suburb of Scarborough to visit some friends. There, they first discussed the idea of simply not going back home. They did, though, and lived to regret it. That night, the footsteps over their heads started up again at about 12:30 AM. And then, once more, the shrieking, cackling laughter like a witch casting an evil spell, "Hee-hee-yeee-hee-hee-hee." As soon as Roy spoke, the sounds immediately stopped. In spite of their heightened state of terror, Carol and Roy did manage to fall into a light, fitful sleep—but not for long. At about four o'clock in the morning, something woke the couple, just in time for both of them to observe their long-haired Persian cat, Fluffy, walk out of their bedroom toward the door to the attic, which was just out of their line of sight. The next thing they knew, there was a resounding thud, as though someone (or something) had hurled the cat against the wall. The cat began to shriek, followed by more shrieking (not the cat), and then the ghostly footfalls began again, once more accompanied by the swelling peal of a witch's cackle. Roy went to investigate.

"Is the cat dead?" Carol called out to him. Fluffy wasn't dead, but the cat was very, *very* frightened. Roy found it huddled against the wall with all of its fur standing on end as it stared intently at the attic door.

Later that morning, Roy dragged himself out the door to his last day of employment before the strike was to begin. Understandably worried, once he was at work, Roy phoned Carol at home to see if everything was all right. She answered the phone in a state—this time, in broad daylight, the phantom footsteps had commenced once more and, even as Carol spoke to Roy on the phone, *a light appeared under the attic door.*

At this point, Carol abruptly hung up and ran out into the suburban sunshine, where she saw their neighbour, Ron Leyzack, weeding his lawn. When she told him her tale of terror, he simply replied that there must be an animal in the attic. She replied that her husband and father had already checked. Leyzack offered to go up to the attic, there and then, armed with his .22-calibre rifle. He did so and found—nothing. He later said that if Carol had told him she had heard footsteps only minutes before, he might not have gone to investigate, rifle or no.

Ron Leyzack also did something else that might not have occurred to most people—he called the *Toronto Telegram* and spoke to two reporters, John Gault and John Downing. The reporters arrived at Prince Edward Drive later that afternoon and met Carol in front of the house. They asked her to show them the apartment and the attic.

"I'm not going up there," she replied. Eventually, though, the two reporters persuaded her to re-enter the house and show them the family's living quarters and the attic. Like Roy Hawkins and Albert Cracknell before them, Gault and Downing could find no tracks, traces or damage that might have been left by an animal. They, too, were forced to admit that the attic appeared to be sealed tight against any would-be intruder from without.

With their curiosity piqued, the two reporters decided to spend Thursday night in the house. Before they settled in for the night in the apartment, they persuaded the Hawkins to sprinkle flour over the floor of the attic to register the steps of anything that might leave footprints. Gault and Downing began their vigil in the darkened apartment around midnight. At about 1:00 AM, they heard indistinct sounds that *could* have been footsteps coming from above them, but nothing definite. At around 3:30 AM, the hatch up to the attic, which weighed nearly 15 kilograms, gave a sort of a thump, followed by sounds that might have been walking. Fluffy the cat also mewed plaintively in the spot where she had been so badly frightened the previous night. By the light of dawn, Gault and Downing could see that there were no footprints or other marks in the flour scattered on the attic floor. As they walked out into the early morning light, the two men were unconvinced.

On Friday, Reverends Pat and Tom Bartlett, a husband-and-wife team from the Star of Progress Spiritualist Church, arrived at the house by invitation from either the Hawkins or the *Toronto Telegram*. Carol explained that she was worried that the disturbances might somehow be connected to little Steven's illness. The Bartletts didn't think so, and Tom went up into the attic to investigate while his wife entered a sort of trance. When Tom returned, he reported the following:

> At the head of the stairs, I stopped and willed whatever it
> was to appear. I saw a brown oval of light—a cocoon.
> Brown means the spirit is still linked to this earth [that is,
> it could have been the spirit of someone still alive]. I think
> the spirit is nearing transition—that's what we call death.
> She must be very ill or has taken a bad turn in her mind.

She has some obsession to come to this place. She probably once lived here and was happy.

Pat Bartlett described a similar experience, saying, "I saw a band of brown light. I then got a terrible pain in my stomach and chest. This person is suffering some serious illness—perhaps cancer." Then, with the two reporters watching every move and recording every word, there was a series of thumps from overhead in the attic. Mrs. Bartlett pointed to a light that had appeared under the attic door, which Gault and Downing also saw. No one appears to have thought of actually going up into the attic to investigate.

Prince Edward Drive: The house as it looks today. As far as anyone knows, subsequent tenants have never reported any paranormal activity.

Despite a midnight exorcism performed by the Bartletts, the disturbances continued. Carol Hawkins fainted after becoming hysterical, and the entire family decamped to the Cracknells' ground-floor apartment. But even there, they got no peace as the spooky tread began once more at 4:00 AM on Saturday, now apparently coming from the very apartment the family had just vacated. Carol's mother, Mrs. Cracknell, reported that she had seen a flash of light at the top of the stairs that led to the apartment and called the Szostak family, who owned and rented the house to the various tenants. She told the two reporters from the *Toronto Telegram*, "We are all petrified now."

For their part, Gault and Downing were slowly becoming convinced that something very strange was indeed happening in the old converted farmhouse. At various times while they were in the house, they saw the mysterious lights everyone else had noticed, later writing that they were spheres about "the size of a half-dollar." They had also learned that, in addition to strange sounds, Carol and Roy Hawkins had also inexplicably experienced a strong scent of perfume in their bedroom. The reporters decided to keep a second watch on Sunday night, joined by Ed Szostak, the son of the landlords. But this time, before they had even settled in for their vigil, the ghostly footsteps started again. Shirley Cracknell, Carol's 10-year-old sister, who lived in the ground-floor apartment with her parents, became hysterical and eventually had to spend the night at her aunt's house. Her mother had a complete breakdown and had to be sedated.

Not to be deterred, Gault and Downing stayed in the house and rigged the attic with an elaborate system of threads and bells that anyone or anything walking around would be sure to trip over, thus ringing the bells. At about 11:00 PM, they turned out the lights and settled down to wait. At about 2:00 AM, the footsteps began in the attic above their heads, slow and clear. The footfalls grew and faded in volume as though whatever it was, was pacing in a circle. After about 10 minutes, the footfalls ceased. None of the bells had been tripped. Neither man went to investigate. At about 3:30 AM, the footsteps began again, and swells of cold air rolled over the two reporters. They estimated that, in a matter of seconds, the temperature in the room dropped by about 30 degrees, from 70°F [21°C] to 40° or 45°F [4° to 7°C]. Again, amazingly, neither of the reporters appears to have made any effort to enter the attic to investigate.

The May 8 appearance of Gault and Downing's first piece in the *Toronto Telegram* brought a new wave of terror to the remaining occupants of the house on Prince Edward Drive in the form of rowdy curiosity seekers. The Hawkins had temporarily moved elsewhere, needing a more stable atmosphere for little Steven's upcoming operation. But the Cracknells and their daughter Shirley remained behind. Having read the article in the newspaper that day, hordes of people descended upon the house, invading the property, incessantly ringing the doorbell and even going so far as to lob projectiles at the house—all in the hope of eliciting a response from either its harried human occupants or its restless spirits. The Cracknells estimated that by the end of the day, hundreds of people had trodden across their lawn.

Meanwhile, Gault and Downing had been diligently digging around in the house's past. They managed to track down William Tomlinson, the great-grandson of the house's original builder. William was the one who had converted the house into a duplex in 1941 and subsequently sold it to the Szostaks. He told the two reporters that his grandparents had also lived in the house, and for the last 15 years of his grandfather's life, the upper floor had never been used, but he didn't know why. While hardly conclusive, this new revelation did add an extra element of mystery to the story.

By the end of May, although the disturbances seemed to have completely stopped, both the Hawkins and Cracknell households had decided to move elsewhere, finding new lodgings together in North Toronto. Besides the Bartletts' theory that the spirit was one of a living person, possibly an old woman, near to death and dying from some form of stomach cancer, no other explanation for the disturbances was ever advanced, either speculative or factual. Certainly *something* unusual was happening in the old house, and the published observations of reporters Gault and Downing lend an air of credibility to events that otherwise beg some kind of natural explanation. However, the reluctance of the two reporters to go up to the attic during the strange occurrences is rather baffling—perhaps they simply didn't want to ruin a good ghost story.

Chapter Nine
The God Helmet

~

Many paranormal experiences are characterized by a feeling of "presence," the hair-raising sensation that someone (or something) is close to you, perhaps peering over your shoulder or standing eerily at the foot of your bed. Others are characterized by a transcendental vision of "God" (whatever God may be for you) or a sense that you have left your body and are entering a different realm. Some people experience physical sensations, as though a spirit or unknown entity is physically pulling them or tugging on a particular limb or part of their body. Amazingly, though, these experiences might also be associated with the earthly agency of an old Ski-Doo helmet with wires and electrodes sprouting out of it like spaghetti bursting through the holes of an overturned colander.

Dubbed the "God Helmet" by overeager media outlets, this remarkable apparatus is the brainchild of Dr. Michael Persinger of Laurentian University in Sudbury. Among many other areas of expertise, Dr. Persinger's research foci include "the electromagnetic correlates of consciousness and experience" and "experimental simulation of mystical and religious experiences within the laboratory." In other words, can fluctuating fields of electromagnetic waves trigger brain functions that cause a subject to believe that someone else is present nearby, or even that she or he is seeing God? The answer would appear to be "yes."

In Dr. Persinger's studies, subjects are seated in a darkened, soundproofed room. Halved table tennis balls are placed over the subject's eyes to block out any possible visual stimuli, and the helmet is put on the subject's head. For the next 30 minutes, electromagnetic impulses are circulated through the electrodes that run through the helmet. Dr. Persinger describes these impulses as "a series of complex repetitive patterns whose frequency is modified variably over time." The output power of these patterns is lower than an electric hair dryer. These patterns of electromagnetic signals mimic the neuron-firing patterns of the brain, thus, in theory, stimulating the brain itself. The results, for some, are remarkable.

Dr. Susan Blackmore, a British professor of psychology at the University of the West in Bristol, England, underwent the procedure as part of a BBC science program called *Horizon*. Later, in an article for the magazine *New Scientist*, Dr. Blackmore reported that she had experienced a sensation "as though two hands had grabbed my shoulders and were bodily yanking me upright. I knew I was still lying in the reclining chair, but someone, or something, was pulling me up." She also wrote that, later during the process, "something seemed to grab hold of my leg and pull it, distort it and drag it up the wall." She also experienced sudden waves of intense anger and fear.

Jack Hitt, a reporter for *Wired* magazine, also subjected himself to the helmet's influence. Although he confessed to being underwhelmed by the experience and baffled by the odd questions asked afterward, Hitt still admitted that he had felt "a distinct sense of being withdrawn from the envelope of my body and set adrift in an infinite existential emptiness, a deep sensation of waking slumber," and later, "there's a separation again, of body and soul, and—almost by my will—I happily allow myself to drift back to the surprisingly bearable lightness of oblivion." He found himself remembering or revisiting happy experiences from his youth, memories he had not recalled in years. In conclusion, he wrote, "Even though I did have a fairly convincing out-of-body experience, I'm disappointed relative to the great expectations and anxieties I had going in."

These two writers are not the only ones to have had remarkable experiences with the so-called God Helmet. Scores of other test subjects have reported sensations ranging from the awe-inspiring to the terrifying. In Dr. Persinger's model, the right and left hemispheres of the brain can react quite differently to the stimuli of the helmet. The right hemisphere, concerned with survival functions, may trigger the perception of an "alien presence" that is threatening or ominous, whereas stimulation of the left hemisphere may produce an experience perceived as divine or pleasantly transcendent.

As the seat of the brain's language centre, the left lobe, when stimulated, can also produce voices or instructions heard by no one but the percipient.

Compelling as they are, Dr. Persinger's findings have yet to be reproduced by other clinicians or confirmed in a peer-reviewed journal. At the same time, so many of his subjects have reported such remarkable experiences that the power of suggestion alone (as some have suggested) does not seem an adequate explanation of the phenomena described. Is it possible that some of humanity's most profound experiences—from revelatory visions to spirit visitations to alien abduction—are simply products of electromagnetic stimulation of the brain? Could the presence of some type of electromagnetic interference have spawned some of history's most mystical and profound episodes of ineffable experience? Could all of the world's religions rest on the firings of a few synaptic connections? The jury is still out on this one and, likely, always will be. For some, a neurophysical "explanation" such as this one might negate the existential awe that normally accompanies such experiences, whereas, for others, the notion that our deepest, most mysterious and affecting perceptions may stem from the brain's inner workings only increases their wonderment at the richness and complexity of the human body. If you feel that someone is looking over your shoulder as you're reading, it could be the living proof.

UFOS AND OTHER MYSTERIES OF THE AIR

Chapter Ten

The Airborne Menace

~

In February 1915, Canada, along with the rest of the British Commonwealth, had been at war for well over a year. With the outbreak of World War I in 1914, Canada had begun a massive mobilization, and boatloads of Canadians were heading overseas to spill their blood in the muddy trenches of Europe. This was a new kind of war—"total war"—in which the entire economic and production capabilities of the participating nations were commandeered for the war effort. Horrible new weapons were used on a wide scale, including tanks, machine guns, aircraft and mustard gas. Near the end of the war, the Germans took to shelling London from occupied Paris with an enormous ordnance piece later known as the "Paris Gun." This behemoth had a 30-metre-long barrel and could lob a shell 120 kilometres across the English Channel, such a vast distance that the firing solutions had to take into account the rotation of the earth while the shell was in flight. Indeed, from the war's outset, no one in either camp knew quite what terrible engines of war the other side might have invented.

Canada, of course, was too far away from the fighting to be under direct threat, but the first Zeppelin bombing raid on London, England, in January 1915 made many people uneasy. Was it possible that the Germans could send a Zeppelin all the way across the Atlantic Ocean to rain bombs down on Canada? Or was it possible that German saboteurs could set up a secret airfield somewhere in North America and launch attacks from there? While unlikely, the fact was that no one knew for sure.

That was why, on the evening of Valentine's Day 1915, residents of Ottawa and the surrounding area were alarmed to see unidentified lights over the city. Planes (or "aeroplanes" as they were still called) were a rarity, and *any* nighttime lights flying over the city would have been noteworthy. At about 9:15 that night, the residents of Brockville, including the mayor and three police officers, looked skyward and were surprised to see the lights of what they presumed to be an unidentified aircraft travelling toward Ottawa across the St. Lawrence River. Many witnesses reported hearing the "unmistakable sounds of a whirring motor."

Soon, another airborne ship was observed, also crossing the St. Lawrence River, apparently from the direction of Morristown, New York. It was seen to drop three "fire balls" (so called by the newspapers) into the river. While some worried that these were bombs, others thought they were flares intended to guide the enemy pilots of the Triple Alliance as they flew toward Ottawa for a bombing run. The mayor said he had also seen one of the ships emit a piercing shaft of light, in the manner of a searchlight, that lit up an entire city block. Witnesses in the east and west ends of Brockville observed two more ships, one passing over each end of the city.

All of these events were observed at or around 9:15 PM. At about 9:30, the mayor of nearby Ganonoque called Brockville's chief of police to report that two unseen but distinctly audible airships had been heard over his city. Soon Prime Minister Robert Borden had been alerted (Borden is the square-jawed, moustache-sporting man on our $100 bills). Borden worried that if some sort of aerial attack was indeed underway, the lights of the Parliament Buildings would be a big, glowing bull's-eye for the enemy raiders, so he ordered the lights turned off. The Parliament Buildings went dark at about 11:15 PM, which was probably alarming for the city's residents. Other high-profile targets, including the Governor General's residence at Rideau Hall and the Royal Canadian Mint, also doused their lights when the rest of Ottawa went dark a few minutes later at 11:20 PM. Watchful snipers were dispatched to the rooftops to shoot down any enemy aircraft that might attack from the darkness.

Other cities in east-central Canada also experienced unusual lights that night. In Toronto, residents reported to police that a "strange aeroplane" had flown over their homes. In Guelph, multiple witnesses watched three glowing lights hover over the agricultural college. There was even a report from as far away as Manitoba—upon hearing a strange noise, three friends looked up into the night sky to see a fast-moving "aeroplane."

But as the grey light of dawn spread over the capital the next morning, the Parliament Buildings were still standing. So were the cities of Ottawa, Brockville and Ganonoque. No more strange airships were spotted, and soon a plausible, if incredible, explanation emerged—for the lights over the Ottawa area, at least. It turned out that some pranksters just across the river in Morristown, New York, had set loose three paper balloons loaded with fireworks. One assumes that they were constructed in the manner of Chinese paper lanterns, heated from within by a small candle or other flame that glowed steadily as they were borne aloft on northerly winds. The onboard fireworks were responsible for the balls of fire, the apparent searchlight and even the whirring sounds thought to be engines. It is difficult to see how a firework could create a whirring sound, other than perhaps the spinning pinwheel variety, but surely these would have been visible, madly rotating as they spewed forth sparks.

The motivation of the American pranksters had been to celebrate the 100th anniversary of the end of the War of 1812. The Treaty of Ghent, which ended the war, had been signed in December 1814 in Belgium, but the news took two months to travel across the Atlantic—the practical jokers in Morristown had been celebrating the cessation of hostilities. In 1915, the U.S. had not yet entered World War I and would not do so until April 1917. One assumes that the merry pranksters of Morristown either did not understand or simply did not care about the implications of sending mysterious airborne objects into a neighbouring country on high alert during a war. Canadians were skeptical that paper balloons alone could have been responsible for everything they had seen, but a police officer actually found two of the deflated paper sacks littering the streets of Brockville, and the explanation seemed to gain some credence and was eventually accepted. Nonetheless, preferring to err on the side of caution, the next night, Ottawa once again went dark at nightfall, and the snipers resumed their rooftop vigils.

The great aerial invasion of 1915 illustrates how dependant our perceptions of mysterious phenomena may be on the circumstances in which we encounter them. Had Canada not been at war, the strange lights would have been greeted with curiosity and possibly even delight—the unknown might have been a source of wonder. If there had been "New Agers" in 1915, they would have thought, "Hooray, the aliens have come to take us away to their planet of rainbows and unicorns. Come in peace, friends." But introduce a mysterious aerial apparition to a nation at war, and the reaction will be considerably different, more along the lines of "We don't know what it is, but it has clearly been sent by the enemy and we must either elude it or destroy it." Sad to say, but during times of war, mysteries cease to inspire wonder and breed fear instead.

Chapter Eleven

Project Magnet

~

As every ufologist knows, the "modern" UFO age began on June 24, 1947. That day, at about 3:00 PM, American businessman and pilot Kenneth Arnold was flying solo to a business meeting in Yakima, Washington. Passing Mount Rainier, he spotted what seemed to be a formation of incredibly bright lights, flying at what he later estimated to be almost 2000 kilometres per hour. He reported the sighting and later described the spinning motion of the objects to a journalist as being "like a saucer skipping across water." Soon though, the press was using the term "saucer" to describe the *shape* of the objects as opposed to their axial spinning motion, and so the age of the "flying saucer" began.

Explanations for what Kenneth Arnold *really* saw have been as diverse as they are unlikely—a meteor breaking up, a flock of pelicans, water droplets on his windscreen, reflections of nearby mountain peaks, clouds and snow flurries. *Whatever* it was that Arnold saw, media accounts captured the public's imagination and soon the terms "flying saucer" and "UFO" had entered the public lexicon. Before long, countless others had also allegedly seen flying saucers, and soon, one was sighted over Canada's capital, Ottawa.

Possibly prompted by their U.S. counterparts, the Canadian military began to seriously investigate the UFO reports they received. The RCAF scrambled fighters to chase any suspicious or unknown craft but had only sporadic and distant visual contact, much less interception or capture. In a move that was typically Canadian in its conciliatory intent, the Defence Research Board (DRB) next decided that perhaps they could coax the aliens into making the first move. And so the DRB implemented a special base just outside Suffolk, Alberta. There, a combination of searchlights and radio signals was used to try to lure UFOs into landing. As far as anyone knows, the aliens are still playing coy.

Enter Wilbert Brockhouse Smith, an electrical engineer from Lethbridge, Alberta, who believed that the earth's magnetic field could be harnessed as a motive energy source to perhaps one day drive planes, trains and automobiles. During the war years, Smith had been in signals intelligence, and afterward, he set up a chain of observation stations across Canada to measure radio waves in the ionosphere, the upper layer of earth's atmosphere.

In 1950, on a business trip to Washington, DC, Smith came upon two early, seminal books about UFOs: *Behind the Flying Saucers*, by Frank Scully, and *The Flying Saucers Are Real*, by Donald Keyhoe. These works put forth the theory that UFOs were powered by electromagnetic energy. With his interest in harnessing earth's geomagnetic force as a means of propulsion, Smith conceived the idea of furthering his research by studying UFOs. He sent a report to the head of the telecommunications branch of the Canadian Department of Transport (DOT) that read, in part:

> *...we are on the track of a means whereby the potential energy of the earth's magnetic field may be abstracted and used....It appeared to me that our own work in geomagnetics might well be the linkage between our [terrestrial] technology and the technology by which the saucers are designed and operated.*

In November 1950, the DOT agreed to earmark a few slender resources to kickstart what was then referred to as Project Magnet, though it was never acknowledged as an official government initiative. Smith found himself with a small staff of three other engineers, besides himself and two technicians. Project Magnet's emphasis quickly shifted from studying the earth's geomagnetic forces *as well as* UFO technology to focusing almost exclusively on UFOs as they related to new technology. The reasons for this shift are not clear, but one possibility is that studying terrestrial geomagnetism with the resources available at that time was simply beyond the scope of the project's capabilities. Another possibility is that harnessing such energy into a practicable propulsion system was quickly discovered to be unworkable (after all, we still haven't done it today). The objective of observing and documenting UFOs became the search for a clue that would act as a sort of Rosetta Stone for earthly engineers to bridge the gap between humanity's crude understanding of electromagnetic propulsion and the aliens' presumed mastery of it.

Meanwhile, the Canadian government had determined that a more unified effort was required to co-ordinate UFO investigation. In early 1952, they struck a committee codenamed Project Second Storey. Second Storey did not last long—from 1952 to 1954—but it did take UFO information gathering very seriously and implemented procedures to standardize the ways that UFO sightings could be reported. Wilbert Smith sat on the committee even as he was working on Project Magnet. In spite of Smith's involvement, though, Project Second Storey eventually concluded that there was no reason to have a formal military investigation into UFO phenomena. Less than a year later, Second Storey was dissolved. To date, it was the Canadian government's only acknowledged formal investigation into UFOs.

Even with the dissolution of Project Second Storey, Project Magnet continued its laudable, if rather vague, work. But soon the initiative's stated goal took a sharper focus. In November 1953, a press release revealed that Wilbert Smith had set up a de facto UFO-spotting station:

> In a few weeks, an observatory, which it is hoped will elucidate the mystery of the flying saucers, will begin its work at Shirley's Bay, about twelve miles from Ottawa.

The laboratory has been equipped with all the instruments now available for that purpose. It will be directed by Mr. Wilbert Smith, Chief Engineer of the Electronics Division of the Canadian Ministry of Transport. Mr. Smith has made the following statement: "There is a good chance that the flying saucers are real objects. The odds are sixty to a hundred that they are extra-terrestrial vehicles."

Smith's public mention of UFOs put a scare into his government minders, and they were quick to point out that although Smith as an individual *was* employed by the government, Magnet was not an official government project, but rather, any personnel, equipment or other resources were simply on loan to Smith. Be that as it may, the Shirley's Bay facility was soon up and running, boasting among its equipment a gamma-ray counter, a magnetometer, a radio receiver and a recording gravimeter. The sophisticated equipment was about to get its first and only workout.

On August 8, 1954, at 3:01 PM, the instruments went haywire, especially the gravimeter. Smith and his staff rushed outside and peered up into the grey, overcast sky, hoping to see heaven knows what. But the cloud ceiling was too low to see whatever was causing the disturbance. Smith later said, "All evidence indicated that a real unidentified flying object had flown within feet of the station."

As soon as the media got wind of this not-very-close encounter, Smith found himself subjected to more pressure from his government handlers, who were now openly embarrassed that the DOT might be associated with a UFO hunter. The project was shutdown shortly afterward. The final press release acknowledged that a lot of data had been collected, but that trying to fit it into any sort of useful pattern had so far proved futile.

Wilbert Smith continued to work for the Department of Transport—he was too able an engineer and scientist to be discarded simply because he held some unorthodox ideas. However, a year after the Shirley's Bay incident, Smith officially testified that the station had *never detected* a UFO, leading some researchers to believe that Smith had finally been muzzled by government pressure.

Smith continue to be highly interested in UFOs, though, and even as he continued his conventional scientific work for the government, he became more and more interested in the "metaphysics" of UFOs. This sprang from the belief that alien life was too complex for humans to understand through science, so Smith began trying other ways of communicating with the supposed occupants of the craft he had so far never seen. He began reading everything he could about people who had been contacted by aliens, even going so far as to investigate a woman who said she communicated with aliens through "automatic writing," which is more often found in séances than in extraterrestrial communication.

Wilbert Smith died from cancer in 1962. At the end of his life, he was superintendent of Radio Regulations Engineering with the Department of Transport. General Electric posthumously awarded him the Lieutenant-Colonel Keith S. Rogers Memorial Engineering Award for dedicated service in the advancement of technical standards in Canadian broadcasting. Smith was one of that rare breed of men with impressive technical and scientific training, but who still possessed enough imagination to admit the possible existence of things he did not completely understand. Smith's work in an orthodox field such as electrical engineering, balanced by his willingness to accept unorthodox beliefs such as automatic writing marked him as an unusual thinker, someone firmly grounded in science yet still open to mystery.

Chapter Twelve

Close Encounters in Ontario

~

Every year since 1989, dedicated Canadian UFO researchers have pooled their resources to produce the Canadian UFO Survey. It documents the number and type of yearly UFO sightings in Canada, using standardized reporting. The numbers show that sightings are increasing each year. In the first year, 1989, there were 141 documented cases, and by 2008, the number had climbed to just over 1000.

The survey uses various criteria to classify the sightings it records. Among these is a modified version of the Hynek Scale, named after its inventor, scientist and ufologist Dr. Josef Allen Hynek (1910–86). Hynek's system classifies sightings or encounters as follows:

Nocturnal Light (NL) is a light source in the night sky;

Nocturnal Disc (ND) is a light source in the night sky that appears to have a definite shape;

Daylight Disc (DD) is an unknown object observed during daylight hours;

Close Encounter of the First Kind (C1) is an ND or DD that occurs within 200 yards [183 metres] of the witness;

Close Encounter of the Second Kind (C2) is a C1 in which physical effects are left or noted;

Close Encounter of the Third Kind (C3) is a C1 in which figures or entities are encountered;

Close Encounter of the Fourth Kind (C4) is an alleged abduction or contact experience.

Hynek's list has been expanded by subsequent researchers to include numerous subtypes and additional categorizations.

All UFO sightings and experiences in Ontario, of course, fall into one of the above categories, but there are so many reports that it is difficult to know where to begin. Therefore, I have chosen to present a "best of" selection—encounters that are particularly notable, had multiple witnesses or observable effects or that received a large amount of media attention. Cast your eyes skyward.

Moose Factory, 1950

Over several months in 1950, strange sights and events were reported by several witnesses in this little community near James Bay. A strange, stationary light, compared by observers to a red traffic signal, was seen hovering over Nemiscau, a trading post on the eastern shore of the bay, in Québec. Nemiscau's factor (the person in charge of a trading post) and his assistant both saw the light and were adamant that it was not a star. First Nations residents also reported two objects with bright lights like airplanes, but suspended motionless in midair. Weirdest of all was the sighting of several "strange white men" who would run away upon being sighted and whom no pursuers could catch. Interestingly, in this case, the fear seems to have been not alien abduction, but rather infiltration by some enemy power of earthly origin such as Russia.

Toronto, 1957

On the evening of November 6, 1957, there were 61 reported UFO sightings across North America. At about 8:00 PM in Toronto, six witnesses saw a yellow light soar over Lake Ontario, moving northward. At the same time, TV interference was also noted. This alone might have been an unremarkable report were it not followed about an hour later by a closer encounter at Lake Baskatong, 160 kilometres north of Ottawa. Some fishermen spotted a bright yellow sphere silently hovering motionless over the peak of a hill that was a few kilometres away. The low-hanging clouds meant that the yellow sphere must have been relatively close to the ground. Single beams of light suddenly shone straight up and down from the object, illuminating the forest below and the cloud ceiling above. An examination through binoculars revealed no additional details—there was just a bright sphere of light emitting two shafts of light, one up and one down. The fishermen then noticed that their battery-powered radio, which had until then been enjoying perfect reception, was now hissing with static. They tried their emergency shortwave radio, and it, too, was one big static hiss, except for one frequency on which there was a single, modulated, electronic pulse that was later compared to Morse code. Otherwise, they could not find a clear channel anywhere on the dial. After a quarter of an hour, the object slowly rose into the clouds and was seen no more. Radio reception returned to normal.

Kenora, 1989

On the evening of November 19, 1989, an unusual sequence of events began in northern Ontario. Kurt Rosentreter was driving east, toward Kenora, on the TransCanada Highway. He was returning from Winnipeg. At about 9:30 PM, he was close to West Hawk Lake and noticed a bright flashing light to the east, just over the trees and perhaps 55 metres off the ground, "I noticed it change direction, move parallel to my car and then toward me, and then it was gone after 20 minutes. It couldn't have been an airplane because it was flashing too inconsistently and could change directions too suddenly."

At 11:30 that night, Joanne Leonard, who lived just outside Kenora, was awoken by the sound of her phone ringing. When she answered it, all she heard was an odd buzzing, so she hung up. Then the phone rang again. Looking out the window, she saw that the streetlights were flashing on and off. Then, to the northwest, she saw a pulsating, red glow, the rhythm of which seemed to match the on-and-off cycle of the streetlights. Mrs. Leonard's television had not been on for hours, but now she saw the screen start to glow as though it had just been turned off.

To the northeast of town, Mrs. Robin Rowe discovered that her bathroom light was repeatedly turning itself on and off. Looking out the window, she reported seeing an object about 30 metres in diameter with a red, pulsating light that reflected off the underside of the clouds. Below her in the valley, she could see the lights of other houses blinking on and off in time with the red, pulsating glow. She tried to call someone to find out what was going on but could hear only a buzzing sound when she picked up the telephone receiver.

Throughout the area, other witnesses reported similar experiences. One person saw a spinning object that emitted an orange light. Between them, the Kenora police and the Ontario Provincial Police (OPP) received nine calls, and the OPP's Crimestoppers line was inoperative, emitting the same strange buzzing sound that was affecting other phones. One OPP officer reported seeing red lights in the sky as the various disturbances were taking place. As the story gained momentum across the country, a headline in the *Winnipeg Free Press* proclaimed, "Hundreds Hear Phones Ringing Off Hook, See Bright, Pulsating Light."

What had happened? Aside from the explanation we *want* to be true, that a massive alien mothership was surreptitiously observing the little community of Kenora and caused electromagnetic disturbances, another solution presents itself, namely, that a massive solar flare (or flares) caused the electromagnetic disturbances. The flashing lights and misbehaving phones are consistent with side effects from solar flares. Solar radiation is also what causes aurora borealis, the northern lights. Solar flare activity occurs in 11-year cycles, and 1989 was very nearly one of the peak years of that particular cycle. Although aurora borealis could, to some degree, explain the pulsing glows seen throughout the area, it would in *no way* account for the various *objects* that different witnesses reported seeing.

Regardless of what was causing the disturbances, imagine how eerie it would be to be woken up by your ringing phone with nothing but static on the other end. Or to observe your household lights, and the streetlights as well, turning themselves on and off, apparently motivated by no human agency. Or to see a distant red glow pulsing in time to the misbehaving lights. The glowing TV screen would be pretty scary, too. This particular UFO occurrence reminds us that, as appealing as mysteries may be, sometimes experiencing one can be downright terrifying.

Chapter Thirteen

The Carp UFO

~

Starting in 1989, UFO researchers scattered across Canada and the U.S. began receiving packages through the mail from an individual who would only identify him- or herself as "Guardian." The contents of each package were roughly the same—documents presumably written and created by Guardian. There was a photocopied picture purporting to show an alien, but, more significantly, there was an account of a UFO that, on the night of November 4, 1989, had allegedly crashed in a farmer's field near Carp, about half an hour's drive from Ottawa.

According to Guardian, after Canadian and U.S. authorities were notified (the document did not say by whom), military black ops helicopters descended upon the crashed vessel and boarded it. Three deceased (and presumably alien) crewmembers were discovered inside. The craft was then taken apart and reassembled for study at a facility in nearby Kanata, and the alien corpses were sent to the University of Ottawa for study.

The document concluded with a lengthy conspiracy rant relating the specifics of a joint Chinese-extraterrestrial conspiracy to take over the world by inserting alien implants up the noses of humans to create a zombie slave race to do the bidding of earth's new Sino-ET overlords—and that's the short version of the story.

Understandably, researchers who received these packages were inclined to regard the whole thing as a rather incompetent attempt at a hoax. Nonetheless, representatives from the Canadian UFO Research Network (CUFORN) wanted to be thorough, so they decided to investigate the story. Toronto-based CUFORN investigator Tom Theofanous was put in touch with Carlton-area local Graham Lightfoot, and the investigation was underway.

The village of Carp sits quietly just outside Ottawa. It most likely got its name from the abundant carp in the nearby Carp River. Before being absorbed into Ottawa proper, this bucolic little community was notable for being the home of the last surviving "Diefenbunker," one of several large, underground shelters designed to allow the Government of Canada to continue to function in the event of a nuclear war. They were designated Diefenbunkers after Prime Minister John Diefenbaker, who ordered their construction. This particular bunker was about to become famous as the site of what came to be known as the "Carp UFO."

Lightfoot worked for the Ontario Federation of Agriculture, so he knew the terrain and the area's residents well. He was also a UFO enthusiast. After a bit of legwork, Lightfoot discovered a witness named Diane Labanek. She averred that, on November 4, 1989, she had seen several helicopters scouring the area with searchlights as though looking for something. Next, Labanek saw a bright, airborne object heading toward a swamp near her property. When asked, another area couple said they had been startled by a bright light that shone suddenly into their bathroom window and down the hallway. Others recalled that dogs and cattle seemed "disturbed" that night. However, many residents interviewed by Lightfoot could remember nothing at all unusual about the night in question.

Lightfoot diligently searched the field and swamp behind Labanek's house and failed to find traces of either a crashed alien ship or the heavy equipment that would have been necessary to disassemble and cart it away. Members of CUFORN's fellow group, the Mutual UFO Network (MUFON), sent investigators from both Ontario and Québec. The MUFON investigators agreed with Lightfoot's conclusion that there was no physical evidence that a UFO or any other type of aircraft had landed in the area they searched. The overall feeling was that someone was hoaxing them. And that was also what Lightfoot told Tom Theofanous, the CUFORN investigator back in Toronto.

So that was the end of it—until October 1991, when Tom Theofanous and other UFO researchers received more packages from Guardian. The packages had no return address, but they did bear an Ottawa postmark. Theofanous' package contained the following:

1) Three playing cards—an ace, king and joker—all bearing handwritten notes;

2) A map of the alleged crash site;

3) A VHS tape labelled "Guardian" with a fingerprint on it;

4) Forged "redacted" documents purporting to be from the Canadian Department of National Defence.

The images on the VHS tape have since become iconically recognizable to UFO believers and skeptics alike. Apparently set in the pitch black of a rural night, the video showed some wavering, seemingly stationary lights on the left side—later purported to be flares—and on the right side, an indistinct, oblong shape with a blinking light on top and additional lights at either end. It could have been a UFO. It could have been a helicopter. For that matter, it could have been a pickup truck. Whatever it was, members of both CUFORN and MUFON thought it was worth following up—*after* the long Canadian winter.

In March 1992, the various parties turned their thoughts once again to the mystery that could be thawing out in Carp that very spring. An American named Bob Oechsler (pronounced *Ex-ler*) called Tom Theofanous at CUFORN. He, too, had received a package from Guardian. Oechsler billed himself as a "former NASA mission specialist" with a great deal of expertise in "visual analysis." He was also a ufologist and gave the impression that he had a lot of experience investigating UFO landing sites. On Oechsler's copy of the VHS tape, there was all the usual footage, as well as an extra couple of minutes of video shot from an angle closer to the purported UFO than on the tape sent to Tom Theofanous. But it was still impossible to tell exactly what the thing was. Oechsler wanted to investigate, so Theofanous called up Graham Lightfoot again to see if he could act as a guide, and the meeting was set for May 10, 1992, in Carp.

The Toronto contingent consisted of Theofanous and several other investigators from both CUFORN and MUFON. On May 10, Mother's Day that year, the little convoy of vehicles dutifully set out. In Ottawa, they met up with Lightfoot, Oechsler and Oechsler's son, and the group went for breakfast. After eating, they went back to Oechsler's hotel room to compare their different copies of the Guardian tapes. This was when some of the assembled party noticed that, for someone who was a supposed expert in video analysis, Oechsler had a lot of trouble connecting Theofanous' video camera to the TV in the hotel room so they could play back the tapes.

Next, the expedition went to search for the crash site. Graham Lightfoot directed the others to a country crossroads and pointed out the direction that the UFO would have been travelling if it had followed the trajectory described by Diane Labanek. Now, Bob Oechsler, who said he had *never* been to Canada before, took the lead in the search for the crash site, driving with his son in their pickup truck *ahead* of the others. He told the rest of the group that he wanted to check the area for electromagnetic anomalies and did this by tossing a couple of compasses in the back of his pickup truck. He asked his son to keep an eye on them from the rear window of the cab as the compasses bounced around on the metal floor of the cargo bed. The CUFORN-MUFON contingent followed behind, holding their compasses level in their hands inside their cars. Suddenly, Oechsler's truck pulled over to the side of the road and stopped. The others followed suit, and Oechsler giddily emerged from the cab and said his son had spotted a strange reading as the compasses slid around on the floor of the cargo bed. The CUFORN-MUFON group had seen nothing on their compasses.

Everyone except Oechsler felt that interviewing some of the locals might be a good idea because they might have heard or seen something that would aid in the search for the actual crash site or, at the very least, confirm that some sort of object had actually passed over the area on November 4, 1989. Oechsler preferred to simply follow Guardian's map, which showed that the UFO was supposed to have landed in a swamp of considerable size and with difficult terrain. The others deferred to

Oechsler, and soon everyone was up to their knees in smelly swamp mud and mosquitoes. The going was hard and hot in the warm spring weather. About halfway into the swamp, the Toronto contingent decided to call it a day. Oechsler and his son decided to keep going even though darkness was falling. It took the others half an hour to make it back to where their cars were parked. They left a note on Oechsler's windshield telling him to meet them at a local restaurant for supper.

Oechsler arrived at the restaurant less than an hour after everyone else, saying he'd found the crash site. The others demurred, replying that there simply hadn't been enough time to find the site, examine it in the failing light, struggle back to the truck through the swamp and then drive to the restaurant. Oechsler just smiled. Later, in the parking lot, Theofanous confronted Oechsler and asked what he was trying to do.

"What's wrong with trying to make a buck?" Oechsler responded. Theofanous replied that there was nothing wrong with trying to make a buck, but that principles and methodologies had to be observed.

"No matter what or how good the story is," said Oechsler, "fifty percent of the people will believe you, fifty percent won't. All you have to care about is the fifty percent that will."

Theofanous backed off and decided to wait and see what Oechsler would do next. Interviewing Diane Labanek was the logical next step, so that evening after supper, the entire contingent showed up on Labanek's doorstep, but Diane and her husband didn't arrive home until 10:00 PM. Everyone agreed that this was far too late for an interview, so they arranged to return the next morning to speak to her.

The members of the Toronto contingent all had jobs to get back to, so they returned to the city, leaving Bob Oechsler and Graham Lightfoot to conduct the interview with Diane Labanek. When Lightfoot had interviewed her three years earlier, Labanek had said that she saw a bright, airborne light travelling toward the swamp on the evening of November 4. Now, she described an additional sighting that had occurred in August 1991. Noticing what appeared to be several flares in her back field, Labanek said she then observed some sort of vehicle with flashing lights and a sort of zigzag pattern on its hull. After about five to eight minutes, the lights of the "craft" went out, soon followed by the flares fizzling out. Shortly afterward, helicopters buzzed the area repeatedly, as though looking for something. Her husband had been out on a milk run at this time, just as he had been during the 1989 sighting. Neither of them investigated the actual landing site after the fact, though Diane said she had set out to do this but turned back halfway when she didn't see anything unusual from where she stood.

Oechsler later returned alone to conduct a second interview with Labanek during which she drew him a diagram that showed the ship—or whatever it was—resting on three blocks. It was identical to a diagram included in the Guardian materials, which she claimed to have never seen before.

The images on Guardian's VHS tapes showed none of these details, though the camera was considerably closer than Labanek's vantage point in her house nearly half a mile away. Upon receiving reports of these interviews, everyone except Oechsler was profoundly skeptical.

Next, Oechsler and Lightfoot investigated the Labaneks' back field for themselves. It was nine months after the alleged landing, with a blustery autumn and a long winter in between. In spite of this, Oechsler immediately found some marks on the ground that he proclaimed were clearly from the landing of the object in the field. Lightfoot, who worked for the Ontario Federation of Agriculture and who had done his fair share of tramping through fields in the area, opined that the markings were identical to the kind of damage that skunks can do when digging for grubs. Undeterred, Oechsler pointed out some nearby bushes that were shrivelled and dried, and he announced that this had clearly been caused by radiation. Lightfoot identified the bushes as junipers and pointed out that after a long, cold winter, juniper bushes always look shrivelled. Oechsler then said he would take soil samples and asked if Lightfoot had anything he could put them in. Lightfoot gave him a few empty film canisters, but was surprised that a self-proclaimed expert field investigator hadn't brought his own containers.

Meanwhile, the CUFORN investigators followed up with the Department of National Defence and learned that on August 19, 1991, there had been helicopter exercises going on in the area, but many miles west of the alleged landing site. If landings were planned for farmers' fields during exercises, permission of the property owner was required. Furthermore, to aid in landings, glowing chemical sticks rather than flares were used.

Back in Carp, Lightfoot and Oechsler visited the Royal Canadian Air Force's Uplands base that July. There, they played the video of the alleged landing of an unidentified "craft" for Colonel Cajo Brando and Major Norm Patterson—again and again. Neither man felt that the images showed a type of helicopter that was used by the Canadian military, but Brando acknowledged it could be a U.S. helicopter that had strayed over the border without alerting Canadian authorities. Later, when representatives from the Canadian Department of Transport viewed the footage, they thought they could make out parts of a helicopter, either a commercially manufactured Sikorsky S-76 Eagle or one of Sikorsky's military models, the UH-60 Blackhawk.

That summer, Oechsler took the steps that brought the case to national and even international attention in the UFO community. He called the producers of the TV show *Unsolved Mysteries* and got them to do a story on the events at Carp. The CUFORN and MUFON investigators believed this move was premature because the only evidence they had was contradictory and shaky at best. But the people at *Unsolved Mysteries* wanted a mystery, and the added appeal of a few minutes of grainy video footage showing a purported UFO was mystery enough. Despite signing an agreement with the producers that forbade him from appearing on any other TV show until at least 30 days after the *Unsolved Mysteries* episode had aired, Oechsler also convinced the UFO TV series *Sightings* to do an episode on the Carp events—both episodes, of course, featured Oechsler as a prominent expert. And, rather oddly, given that the star witness, Diane Labanek, had stated she had no interest in UFOs, one of the TV crews that was shooting a scene in her basement discovered stacks of books about just that. Over the next several months, Oechsler and Labanek appeared on several local TV and radio programs, each time professing to know of other witnesses to the events but never able to supply them or even remember their names. Oechsler also went on the UFO lecture circuit in the U.S. and Canada.

Meanwhile, Graham Lightfoot learned that Diane Labanek had a friend named Bobby Charlebois who was interested in UFOs—he was also known to use the name "Guardian." Lightfoot and Oechsler decided to see if they could get Charlebois' fingerprints in order to compare them to the prints on the original VHS tapes they'd received from Guardian. First, they arranged for a local reporter to send Charlebois an envelope full of photos and other material relating to the case, but it was returned unopened later the same day. Next, they asked Diane Labanek to visit Charlebois socially to see if she could get a glass he'd been drinking out of, but Labanek said he always wiped his glasses clean.

As 1992 ebbed into 1993, Oechsler convinced Labanek to request a formal investigation by the RCMP to determine whether government helicopters had buzzed her property so closely in August 1991 that they had blown shingles off her house. It should be pointed out that helicopters flying under the minimum 500-foot (152-metre) ceiling set by the government, especially any flying low enough to blow shingles off houses, would have been audible to Diane Labanek's neighbours as well, but none of her neighbours had reported hearing anything. The stated purpose of the resulting RCMP investigation was the following:

> A: Ascertain if sufficient evidence was available to support a prosecution under the Aeronautics Act, Section 534(2)(b) for flying below 500 feet;
>
> B: Ascertain if in fact the object observed was an aircraft;
>
> C: Ascertain if the craft observed (by complainant) was a UFO (as per complainant).

After an extremely thorough investigation, the lengthy RCMP report concluded as follows:

> A. Not enough evidence was brought forward to support a prosecution under Section 534(2)(b) of the Aeronautics Act;

B. The object observed was a helicopter but could not
be identified because of a lack of sufficient details,
i.e., markings;

C. See B above.

But there is yet another possibility—the object in the
video could be a pickup truck with a flashing red light on top.
The investigators learned that in October 1990, a full 10 months
before the reported landing, Labanek's nephew, Pavel Farfara,
met a property inspector near his aunt's property and spun
a lengthy tale of army involvement with the UFO that had
allegedly landed on his aunt's property. He also happened to
own a pickup truck similar to the model that the CUFORN-
MUFON investigators thought might be the one in the video.

This is the condensed version of the Carp UFO caper.
Readers wishing to do additional research can learn about the
hilariously homemade signs on the Labanek property reading,
"Defence Canada," "Killing Fields" and "Testing Ground," all
hand-lettered in a script similar to that in the original Guardian
materials, and one proudly bearing the word "nuclear" mis-
spelled "nucleear." There was also Oechsler's intrigue regarding
supposed strontium deposits in the soil, proving that military
flares had been lit there, though he did not release the chemistry
report that disproved this for well over a year. There were countless rebuttals, averrals and denials—and even threatened law-
suits—all for naught.

The fact that, even today, the Carp case still generates controversy, drawing both adherents and opponents, shows how strongly we are drawn to the unknown. As more and more of the world's mysteries are solved, the places where true mystery can be found become fewer and fewer. For example, we now know that, during Richard Nixon's Watergate scandal, the infamous informant "Deepthroat," whose identity remained a secret for more than 30 years, was actually FBI Associate Director Mark Felt. The location of the wreck of the *Titanic* has been known for so long now that it's difficult to remember a time when discovering its location was the Holy Grail for underwater explorers. The ongoing relevance of the Carp UFO is not that it provided even the flimsiest proof of an alien landing, but that it still promises mystery, intrigue and possibility in a world sorely lacking in wonder.

Chapter Fourteen

Still Closer Encounters

~

In the earlier chapter "Close Encounters in Ontario," we looked briefly at cases that illustrate various sorts of night-time sightings all the way through to Close Encounters of the Second Kind, in which physical effects are left or noted (for the sake of argument, we shall include the Carp case as a Close Encounter of the First and Second Kinds). Now we shall look at a case that exemplifies Close Encounters of the Third and Fourth Kinds. Just one case? Well, yes, because even in Ontario, there have been so many reported abductions and encounters involving aliens or "entities" that readers seeking a more complete account of these are encouraged to consult the sources listed at the back of this book under the heading for this chapter. The case you are about to read about is instructive because in many ways, it exemplifies a "typical" abduction by aliens or other entities.

Before we start, it is important to distinguish between so-called UFO "contactees" and UFO "abductees." Persons reporting that they have been visited by aliens or "entities" are termed contactees. The entities often appear at the bedside of the percipient with some sort of message to impart, usually important advice that may help to save the earth from humanity's polluting transgressions. Or these entities may communicate telepathically. For the most part, contactees, more so than abductees, feel that they have been chosen for some special purpose or mission—to spread a message of some sort.

On the other hand, abductees report that they have been taken onboard an alien craft and often subjected to some sort of invasive medical test, operation or procedure. They may or may not consciously remember the experience and may suffer from serious and debilitating conditions afterward—agitation, nervousness, panic attacks and even post-traumatic stress disorder. For the most part, the experience is not a positive one, and the abductee may be reluctant to tell others of the experience because of fear of being perceived as crazy. The case of Veronica, outlined below, has characteristics of *both* an abduction *and* a contact.

~

In 1985, Veronica was a young woman in her 20s living just outside Toronto. When her encounters began, she was living in a ground-floor apartment in a busy, populated area. Shortly before sunrise one morning, a small ship landed in the alley behind her apartment. It took up two parking spaces, was about the length of a standard limousine and made a whooshing sound when it took off. The occupants were of the alien type now known as "greys," with large heads and eyes that sort of wrapped part way around their heads. However, they shielded themselves from observation by telepathically projecting a human appearance. They also preserved their collective anonymity by using mass auto-suggestion on any potential witnesses driving or walking through the area. They used a similar method to prevent slumbering neighbours from awakening at an inopportune moment.

The greys took Veronica aboard their ship and conducted a veritable battery of tests and procedures on her. The entities relieved a kidney complaint of Veronica's by "cutting between the cells" (which is why there was no visible scar), curing the disorder and inserting a small implant (which was subsequently flushed through her urinary tract after being observed by an ultrasound technician) to ease the pain. During one abduction (remember, there were many), a female alien harangued Veronica regarding the shocking manner in which humans "spill our seed, pollute our atmosphere and treat others with disrespect." (It has often been noted that aliens appear to subscribe to a more or less Christian ethos.)

In still other abductions, Veronica observed the aliens removing sperm and eggs from captive humans. Indeed, during one visitation, the aliens removed Veronica's own ova for observation. Another time, she was shown adult-sized human bodies grown in vats, taking a mere four days to reach "maturity." The aliens informed her that the bodies contained no spirit. Veronica protested this, but the aliens countered with the simple rebuttal that humans do the same thing to animals. She was also shown alien-human hybrid children. She met another woman named Ellen Robertson who said she was a missing person from Rhode Island.

Initially unable to remember her experiences, Veronica recalled them spontaneously, without hypnosis, when she suffered another harrowing experience—a miscarriage. Although initially afraid to talk about her experiences, Veronica later began to speak publicly about what had happened to her. She has since become a "part-time Christian minister." Whether or not she is still taken onboard alien ships is unknown.

~

Over years of interviews and research, American UFO researcher Budd Hopkins (1931–2011) drew up a list of characteristics common to many abduction experiences. The following summary is taken from an article that appeared in *Saturday Night* in the June 1995 issue:

- An abduction can occur with little or no conscious recall on the part of the abductee.

- Almost invariably, the same individuals are taken numerous times, at irregular intervals, over the course of decades. The abductee becomes, in effect, a tagged animal.

- A "cell-sampling" operation is often inflicted, leaving scars of two types: a round, shallow depression, or "scoop mark," or a long, thin, scalpel-like cut.

- The [aliens'] central focus is the study and laboratory use of human beings, with special attention to our physical, genetic and reproductive properties.

- Members of the same family are often abducted in what seems to be a longitudinal genetic study or experiment.

- Apparently [there is] a systematic attempt to create a hybrid species, a mix of human and "alien" characteristics.

- Widespread artificial-insemination techniques result in human pregnancies; the pregnant women are abducted again to remove the developing embryos, which are then "grown" in laboratories or nurseries within the UFOs themselves.

- The final event involves the re-abduction of the ostensible human "mother"—or sometimes the father—so the human can hold the infant or child in a sort of bonding procedure.

- The alien personality seems to lack emotions. The aliens seem interested in acquiring, or at least understanding, the basic human emotional spectrum.

Hopkins was also a firm believer in the value of hypnotic regression to find out what "really" happened during purported alien abductions such as Veronica's. For many years, Hopkins' supporters pointed out that in some cases, female subjects seeking hypnotic regression to deal with childhood sexual molestation had uncovered alien abduction experiences for which molestation was merely a "screen" memory, used as a subconscious coping method to avoid the original memory. This, they said, showed that far from being an unreliable or "leading" method, hypnosis was clearly the best way to discover what had "really" happened to alleged UFO abductees or anyone else who chose regression to retrieve some lost or blocked memory.

But as the 1990s dawned, the opinion of the professional psychiatric community regarding hypnotic regression began to shift. Numerous clinical studies and trials had shown that, far from being in a state during which subjects would tell only the truth, the whole truth and nothing but the truth, subjects of hypnotic regression were actually in a highly *suggestible* state. Under hypnosis, they could be prone to confabulation, and their responses could be affected by leading questions from the therapist or by some other external influence experienced *before* they were hypnotized.

In mid-1989, Toronto psychotherapist Dr. David Gotlib was contacted by an abductee who had randomly chosen him from the register of the Ontario Society of Clinical Hypnosis. The woman had approached various therapists, but none of them would see her when they discovered that the insomnia, anxiety and nightmares that plagued her were associated with a UFO abduction experience she believed she had undergone. Dr. Gotlib was less concerned with *what* had caused the woman's trauma than with treating its effects—in other words, she was clearly experiencing great emotional difficulty, and regardless of what its root was, Gotlib felt that she deserved to be treated.

In a 1993 interview for *Omni* magazine, Dr. Gotlib summarized his position by saying, "I don't expect to solve the puzzle or have the puzzle solved in my lifetime. These kinds of things have been going on for hundreds of years. I think if we start trying to solve the question definitively, then we're chasing our tail. What I'm most concerned about is, how can we help these people?" His approach is at odds with many UFO investigators, who not surprisingly, are more concerned with what "really" happened than with treating its after-effects.

Some UFO investigators are trained in hypnotism, but they are rarely trained psychotherapists. In the mid-1990s, Dr. Gotlib found himself at the centre of a schism in the UFO world when he advocated for a code of ethics in treating individuals who had experienced alien abduction, including the recommendation that they should only be treated by trained mental-health professionals. Needless to say, this notion was not warmly received by the wider community of UFO investigators, the majority of whom, as we have already pointed out, are not trained psychotherapists.

Nevertheless, in the U.S., the 1990s also saw the formation of a group of clinicians and scientists called TREAT, for Treatment and Research of Experienced Anomalous Trauma. But even among highly accredited practitioners such as these, there is dissent as to what really happens when someone reports an abduction experience—some feel that there are always earthly causes for abduction experiences, whereas others think there could be aliens, and still others admit they simply have no explanation for what the abductees have experienced.

For his part, Dr. Gotlib found that with his first patient, the woman who had been refused treatment by other psychotherapists, after using traditional therapeutic methods, the source of her trauma turned out to be purely earthbound. And, in another case, although the woman's abduction experiences did not cease altogether, they greatly lessened after therapy with Dr. Gotlib, which also eased the patient's anxiety and stress.

By 1995, Dr. Gotlib had about 70 clients (about five percent of his overall patient base) whom he was treating for UFO-related ailments, in some cases even full-blown post-traumatic stress disorder. Interviewed that same year for an article in *Saturday Night*, Gotlib said, "I lean towards the 'imaginal' theory put forth by Ken Ring."

He was referring to Ken Ring, an American psychology professor whose term "imaginal" described phenomena that were very different from merely "imaginary." Imaginal experiences take place while the subject is in a state similar to a lucid dream—the experiences are real to the percipient but may be purely subjective and not observable by anyone else.

There are, not surprisingly, a myriad of diagnosable psychiatric disorders and even physiological states that may explain a good many abduction experiences. For instance, in "sleep paralysis," a person's eyes are open and his or her consciousness is awake, but the voluntary muscle system is not activated and the person cannot move. This combined with hallucinations associated with different parts of the sleep cycle can create an incredibly vivid "visitation experience."

But for Dr. Gotlib, the emphasis was on helping patients to either cope or move beyond the traumatic after-effects of their complaints. He found that after helping patients deal with the terrifying nature of their memories, what often happened was that the experience itself then became imbued with a transcendent or visionary aura. One patient said that the aliens had been trying to tell her "to get off my ass...and do something with my life." Gotlib said that when abduction experiencers could see the events as having some larger meaning, "the experiences slow down, decrease in frequency, and, with some people, stop altogether."

Dr. David Gotlib eventually moved into other areas of psychotherapy, but his approach was a humane and productive one, disallowing neither the percipients' anomalous experiences nor the very real pain and anxiety that these experiences caused. Of course, this chapter must end with a cautionary notion for UFO believers and skeptics alike. In the same *Omni* article in which Dr. Gotlib appeared, Harold Goldstein, a psychologist in the epidemiological and services research branch of the U.S. National Institute of Mental Health said, "Truth should not be defined by what people believe. Facts are facts. Now it may turn out that there are aliens and such things, but there needs to be evidence for it, and belief is not evidence."

CRIMES, DISAPPEARANCES AND DISCOVERIES

Chapter Fifteen

The Kinrade Murder

~

The Kinrades of Hamilton were a prosperous and well-respected family. They lived in a large, comfortable home on Herkimer Street, in one of the city's solid residential neighbourhoods. The father, Thomas L. Kinrade, was a local school principal and owned some 30 houses in the Hamilton area, which he let to renters. The mother, referred to only as "Mrs. Kinrade" in newspaper accounts, appears to have been a typical upper-middle-class matron of the period. There were five children: two adult sons, Earnest and Earl, who had moved away to strike out on their own, and three daughters, Ethel, Florence and Gertrude. Ethel and Florence were both in their 20s, while Gertrude was just 16 and still in school.

Ethel, the eldest, had always lived at home, as had Gertrude. The middle daughter, Florence, was a striking beauty of "Spanish" good looks. She had just returned from a lengthy stay in Richmond, Virginia, where her parents believed she had been singing with a church choir. In the aftermath of the murder, no one found any reason to believe that relations between the various family members were anything other than warm and affectionate.

The only jarring note in this staid, idyllic existence appears to have been the ongoing presence of neighbourhood tramps, who often knocked at the doors of prosperous homes looking for handouts. On the night of February 24, 1909, one such tramp rang the front doorbell of the Kinrade home. The family sometimes gave food and small amounts of money to tramps, but in this case, they did not answer the door, so the tramp repeatedly rang the bell and then tried to pry open a window.

Ethel Kinrade

The next day, February 25, the family convened at home for lunch as they did every day, but by four o'clock that particular afternoon, one of them would be dead.

Because of the events that had occurred the previous evening, it was decided that Mrs. Kinrade would go to the police station and ask for a watch to be placed upon the house to safeguard the family against unwanted intrusion by tramps. After lunch, Thomas and Gertrude returned to school, Mrs. Kinrade left for the police station, and Ethel and Florence cleared away the dishes.

Florence Kinrade

At about ten past three, Ethel and Florence decided to go for a walk and set about getting ready to leave the house. The testimony of two separate witnesses later suggested that the murder and its surrounding events all occurred within about 15 minutes, between 3:40 and 3:55 PM.

Both sisters were upstairs in their respective bedrooms preparing to leave when Florence discovered that one of her gloves had a hole in it, so she went down the back stairs of the house to get a needle and thread. While Florence was downstairs, the doorbell rang. She opened the door to discover a man later described as being about 40 years old, of medium build with a heavy, brown moustache and wearing dark clothes. He wore a dark overcoat and a fedora tilted low over his face. His clothes were rough enough that he was clearly not a gentleman, but not so rough that one would describe him as a tramp. When the stranger asked Florence for food, she replied, "Certainly," and started to close the door, whereupon the stranger stuck his foot in the door and said, "I want all the money you have in the house."

Here, the thread of the story becomes hopelessly tangled. According to the Kinrades' neighbour, Mrs. Frank Hickey, Florence burst breathlessly into the Hickey home declaring, "Ethel is shot—shot six times," though it would later prove to be seven. Florence then said that when the burglar tried to force his way in, Ethel came downstairs to help and the burglar emptied his pistol into her. However, at the inquest (and later), Florence's story changed considerably. She claimed that she had gone upstairs to get $10 to give to the burglar and, passing her sister's room, had told Ethel to lock herself in, but she did not wait to see if Ethel did so. While she was still looking for the money, she heard "a noise like the house going up." Incredibly, in this version of the story, it did not occur to Florence that the sound could have been a pistol shot (or shots), so she went back downstairs to find the burglar standing by the telephone, and she gave him the $10 bill. According to Florence, a nightmarish struggle with the burglar followed. It was nightmarish not least for Florence's inability to remember specific details or to explain why she had acted the way she did.

In some versions of Florence's retelling, she said she tried to escape out a window, but the burglar grabbed her and held her back. Somehow she escaped into the backyard, where she found she was too frightened to call for help and was unable to climb over a knee-high picket fence to get away. Inexplicably, she went back into the house, where she encountered the burglar again and saw Ethel's body lying in a pool of blood. Florence then dashed past the burglar and out the front door to Mrs. Hickey's.

Whatever the truth may have been, one thing was for certain—Ethel Kinrade was lying dead in a pool of her own blood, shot seven times in the head and chest. The shots to her chest had been fired from such a close range that the material of her blouse was singed. The medical examiner later concluded that approximately 15 minutes had elapsed between the first

shots to Ethel's head and the subsequent shots to her chest—[1]
puzzling to say the least.

The press had a field day. Emblazoned across the front
page of the next day's *Hamilton Spectator* was the massive headline, "WHO SHOT ETHEL KINRADE?" The newspapers
also made much of the alleged tramp problem, and for a short
time, public outrage was rallied (or created) by such dire head-
lines as "Ways of Getting Rid of the Tramp Nuisance." But it
would be another two weeks before reporters got their fill. With
both his daughter and wife in a state of nervous prostration (that
is, incoherently hysterical), Thomas Kinrade took them to
a Toronto hotel to allow them to calm down.

The inquest, when it was held two weeks later, tended to
cast Florence in a suspicious light, and not merely for the incon-
sistencies of her story. It emerged that during her time in Virginia, as well as singing with a church choir, she had also taken
to the stage, performing "illustrated songs" at not one, but *two*
different vaudeville theatres, the Orpheum and the Pastime.
Furthermore, she went by the stage name "Miss Mildred Dale"
and had concealed her real name from all of her colleagues there.
While initial reports suggested that her family was unaware she
was performing in vaudeville, her father later told reporters, "We
were fully informed of what she was doing and acquiesced."
However, later testimony by Florence herself confirmed that she
had written misleading letters to her family saying that she was
singing at domestic social events of the day, known as "at homes,"

as well as in church concerts. All the while, she was *also* performing at the Orpheum and the Pastime.

Further muddying the waters was Florence's ambiguous engagement to a Hamilton seminary student named Montrose Wright. As far as her parents were concerned, Montrose and "Flossie," as the papers called her, were engaged to be married. But soon after Florence's return from Richmond, Mrs. Kinrade was alarmed to intercept a letter and gift addressed to one "Mildred Dale." It quickly became apparent that, during her time in Richmond, Florence had entered into a romantic relationship with a Virginian actor-mechanic named James Baum. Mrs. Kinrade hurriedly wrote Baum a letter explaining that Florence was spoken for and she must, perforce, request him to cease and desist in his romantic correspondence with her. The prosecution was able to show that, in her letters to Baum, Florence had been in the habit of making up people who didn't exist—a "Mrs. Marion Elliot," a "Colonel Warburton," a "Kenneth Browne" and a couple named "Foster."

Baum travelled from Virginia to Hamilton to testify at the inquest. He reported that Florence had told him her parents had forced her into an unhappy marriage, but she was now divorced. Furthermore, Baum had proposed to her and, indeed, until recent events, he was under the impression that he and Florence were engaged. As if this weren't enough, Florence had also responded to what was then known as a "matrimonial advertisement" in one of the local newspapers and was writing to a man known only as "Harold." Florence maintained that these post-office dalliances were merely "jokes." One night while performing in Virginia, a huge bunch of flowers was thrown onto the stage at her feet. She read the card but would not tell anyone, even Baum, who the flowers were from, fuelling speculation that she had yet another lover in Richmond. Finally, it emerged that, like many other women at the time in Virginia, Florence was known to carry a revolver when she went about— for protection against "the negroes." She steadfastly swore that she had disposed of the gun before returning to Canada, and diligent searches of both the Kinrade home and their Toronto hotel room failed to turn up any trace of a pistol.

The defence correctly, but still rather unconvincingly, asked what relevance Florence's conduct in Virginia had to the murder of her sister in Hamilton. Likely out of deference to Florence's gender, the family's social standing and the general mores of the time, the coroner's court sided with the defence. There was also a general consensus among the press, the public and the legal types that, although Florence appeared to be neurotic, highly strung, squirrelishly skittish and a bald-faced liar, there just wasn't any evidence that she had murdered her sister, nor was there ever any motive given for why she would have wanted to do so.

By this time, after spilling barrels of ink and besmirching forests of newsprint, the press seemed to tire of the story. The overall sense of public fatigue can be read in a little witticism that appeared on the front page of the *Hamilton Spectator* on

May 5, 1909. Under the headline "Pertinent and Impertinent" is a collection of short jokes, starting with this one, apparently recounting a conversation between two Irishmen overheard on a street corner:

> *"An' so they're finished the inquest,' Jawn; and phwat was the verdic'?*
>
> *Jawn—Begorra, there's the paaper; yez* kin rade *it for yir-self, sure."* [Author's emphasis]

Florence reportedly married the seminary student who had stood by her throughout the ordeal of the inquest. Accounts say they had two children, but when her husband died, Florence once more took to the stage to support them. The rest of the Kinrade family moved away from Hamilton, and nothing more is known of them.

As if fate were doggedly trying to provide closure to this unsolved case, we have an intriguing epilogue in the case of Edward William Bedfort. In October 1909, eight months after Ethel Kinrade's murder, Bedfort, a Canadian, turned himself into the New York police, confessing that he had murdered Ethel. The police duly arrested him and investigated but could not turn up a single shred of evidence that his story was true. Upon further interrogation, Bedfort admitted that his initial confession was, in fact, false and he was released into the obscurity of history—along with whatever information he might have had about the Kinrade case.

Chapter Sixteen

The Death of Tom Thomson

~

I n recent years, the mysteries surrounding Tom Thomson's death and burial have tended to overshadow his remarkable work as a painter. In *Tom Thomson: The Silence and the Storm*, published in 1977 for the centennial of Thomson's birth, fellow painter Harold Town wrote that the impact, importance and greatness of Thomson's work is often overlooked by "art ghouls and plain fools who have turned his creative odyssey into the pedestrian plot for a drug rack paper-back." Since the present writer is quite aware that readers may have purchased this volume in the impulse-buy section of the local marina, I shall tread carefully and offer a bit of background before delving into the undeniably lurid details of Tom Thomson's demise and subsequent exhumation.

~

Tom Thomson was born into a prosperous family on August 5, 1877. Shortly after his birth, the family, which would eventually grow to include nine children, moved from Claremont to Leith, on Georgian Bay. As a boy, Tom enjoyed outdoor activities such as hunting, fishing and sports. As a young man, he struggled to find some sort of "respectable" profession and thought he would perhaps follow one of the responsible career paths his four elder brothers had taken. Drifting from job to job, he began to develop his natural talent for drawing and painting. Soon Thomson found work in commercial engraving and illustration houses. After a three-year stint in Seattle, getting steadily better jobs, he returned to Canada in 1904 and, at the age of 27, finally took some painting lessons. A few years later, he joined the Toronto commercial art firm of Grip Limited and soon earned a reputation as an excellent letterer. Also employed at Grip were several kindred spirits, other artists searching for a vision, and Thomson quickly struck up friendships with these men. Later, following their department head to the new firm of Rous and Mann Limited, Thomson and his colleagues gathered more paint- ers into their little fraternity and, minus Thomson himself, these were the artists who would form the Group of Seven in 1920.

In 1912, Thomson took his first trip to Ontario's far north and, later that same year, to Algonquin Park. On these journeys, Thomson truly found his "voice" as a painter. With the forces of "modern art" on the rise—Picasso, the Dada movement and others—Thomson looked back for inspiration to the Impressionists of the late 19th century. The Impressionists, of course, had painted scenes of the sun-dappled European countryside and its garish city nights. But Thomson and com- pany had for their canvas the immense wilderness of Canada. Brash brushstrokes could make one *feel* the wind as it raced across the rocks and trees of the Great Lakes shoreline. Simple shapes and shadings could help one *hear* the stillness of a winter afternoon in the forest. Splotches of vibrant colour could transmit the very *smell* of autumn leaves underfoot with a mosaic of fall foliage ahead. For people who have been to such places, seeing a Thomson or a Group of Seven canvas is a surprisingly sensory experience, often difficult to explain to city-dwellers or newcomers to Canada.

On his trips, Thomson would dash off dozens of "sketches"—oil paintings on small canvases that he would develop into full-sized paintings back in Toronto. The first of these fully fledged works, *A Northern Lake*, was purchased by the Government of Ontario in 1913 for $250. This was at a time when Thomson's day job paid the respectable wage of 75 cents per hour, or $30 a week. Thomson the painter had arrived.

Over the next four years, until his death in 1917, Thomson's star was on the rise. Although he continued to do commercial work in Toronto during the winter, he spent the rest of the year living at Algonquin Park's Canoe Lake. There he painted, canoed, fished and apparently drank quite a bit. Then, when the last leaves had fallen and lay silvered with frost, Thomson would pack his summer's worth of sketches and head back to Toronto, where he worked them up into full-sized canvases in between commercial contracts.

With each passing spring and summer, Thomson settled more fully into life at Canoe Lake. Although the area had once boasted a bustling little village known as Mowat, changes in the lumber industry meant that the town had suffered a downturn in its fortunes. Greatly reduced in population, Canoe Lake's residents built what industry they could upon seasonal tourism. Park Ranger Mark Robinson was a constant presence and kept detailed journals from which much of the information concerning Thomson's final days has been gleaned.

Mowat Lodge, what today might be called a "resort," was run by the husband-and-wife team of Shannon and Annie Fraser. It was there that Thomson usually stayed, and he was quite friendly with both of the Frasers, taking his meals in the back kitchen of the lodge and even helping out with chores and repairs, possibly for a reduction in board. Thomson also encouraged several of his artist friends from Toronto to come and stay at Mowat Lodge, thus providing additional income for the Frasers. After the National Gallery of Canada bought his painting *Northern River* in 1915 for $500, Thomson even loaned Shannon Fraser $250 to buy some new canoes for the use of lodge guests.

In addition to the year-round locals and vacationing visitors, many families owned cottages on the lake and spent their summers there. Among these was the Trainor family. Hugh Trainor worked for the nearby Huntsville Lumber Company, and though he didn't earn a princely wage, he did make enough to purchase a former park ranger's cabin renamed "The Manse." Hugh and Margaret Trainor had two daughters, Winnifred, aged 27 in 1912 when the Trainors bought the cottage, and Marie, a few years younger.

In 1913, Winnifred met Tom Thomson, and the two of them were soon romantically involved. Although there are varying opinions as to how seriously Thomson viewed the relationship, the Trainors seem to have welcomed the painter into their midst, giving him the use of their cabin when they were not there. Certainly, at 28, Winnie was approaching the age of spinsterhood. For his part, Thomson went into Huntsville often to see Winnie, even when her family was not at Canoe Lake. They were well known in the lumber town and were often seen going about together. Oddly, though, none of the future Group of Seven, who often stayed at Mowat Lodge, ever made mention of Winnie, leading some to speculate that Thomson never introduced her, either because he viewed her as "provincial" or because he himself didn't take the relationship seriously.

This little lakeside community, then, is the backdrop for what happened next, and its denizens are the principle cast members for the tragedy that unfolded.

~

On the evening of Saturday, July 7, 1917, there was a loud, alcohol-soaked party at the cabin of one George Rowe. There, Thomson is alleged to have gotten into an argument with local Martin Blecher Jr. The two men may have quarrelled over the progress of the war or some other point of contention, but they were apparently only halted from fisticuffs by the intervention of cooler, but no more sober, heads. This was the last time Tom Thomson can be reliably said to have been alive.

There are two separate reports of people having seen him the next day, July 8, but both of these are highly questionable. On Monday, July 9, Thomson's canoe was found floating upside down on the lake, empty except for some camping provisions that were tightly strapped in. There was no doubt it was Thomson's canoe—he had extravagantly mixed expensive blue artist's pigment with marine paint to colour the entire canoe a distinctive blue-tinted shade of pale grey known as "dove."

By Tuesday, July 10, the local residents had become involved. Two days later, on July 12, Shannon Fraser, the proprietor of Mowat Lodge, sent telegrams to the Thomson family informing them that Tom's canoe had been found afloat and that he was missing. Park ranger Mark Robinson reported the disappearance to the Algonquin Park superintendent and, along with his son, began hiking all of the trails Thomson was known to frequent, but they found nothing. Tom's brother, George, the family emissary, arrived on Thursday morning and only stuck around for two days before gathering up all of his brother's sketches and paintings and taking them away with him. The newspapers had gotten hold of the story now, with various reports saying that Thomson was missing or likely drowned.

Finally on Monday, July 16, Dr. Goldwin Howland, a vacationing neurology professor from the University of Toronto, was on the front steps of his cabin and noticed something rise to the surface of the lake just a few metres out. He called to some passing canoeists to paddle over to investigate, and so the body of Tom Thomson was discovered. The corpse was bloated and the flesh was beginning to tear in places. The face was unrecognizable, but the hair and clothes marked the body as Thomson's. There was also a considerable length of fishing line wound neatly and deliberately around the left ankle.

Dr. Howland's affidavit read as follows:

I saw body of man floating in Canoe Lake Monday, July 16, at about 10:00 AM and notified Mr. George Rowe, a resident, who removed body to shore. On 17th Tuesday, I examined body and found it to be that of a man aged about 40 years in advanced stage of decomposition, face abdomen and limbs swollen, blisters on limbs, was a bruise on right temple size of 4" [10 centimetres] *long, no other sign of external marks visible on body, air issuing from mouth, some bleeding from right ear, cause of death drowning.* [Mark Robinson's journals said that the wound or gash was actually on the left side of the forehead, and Dr. Howland later agreed.]

The series of misadventures that befell the body of Tom Thomson over the next few days and, indeed, over the next few decades, are something of a mystery themselves. Greatly abbreviated, the sequence of events was as follows: Algonquin Park superintendent George Bartlett telegraphed to North Bay to request that coroner Dr. Arthur Ranney come down to conduct a proper autopsy. In the meantime, though, either Shannon Fraser or Mark Robinson suggested a quick burial in the park itself and superintendent Bartlett agreed, signing the necessary papers. Dr. Howland, as the only medical man present, signed a death certificate giving the cause of death as drowning. The painter's body was then taken out to a small island, where it was embalmed as ranger Robinson and Dr. Howland looked on. Winnie Trainor arrived, demanded to see the body and was refused. Thomson's remains were then placed in a wooden casket and buried in the park after a small ceremony.

Meanwhile, Winnie, in touch with the Thomson family, had learned that they had wanted their son's body buried in the family plot in Leith, near Owen Sound. Telegrams to this effect sent by the Thomsons to Shannon Fraser either never arrived or were ignored. Winnie set about making arrangements for an undertaker from Huntsville—a Mr. Churchill—to travel to Canoe Lake, exhume the body, transfer it to another casket and see that it was conveyed to the Thomson family in Owen Sound. Then Winnie took a train back to Huntsville. Several hours *after* Thomson had been buried at the park, the coroner arrived from North Bay and concurred with Howland's verdict of death by drowning without ever having seen the body, which was now lying beneath several feet of earth.

Thomson had been buried at Canoe Lake on July 17. On the evening of July 18, Mr. Churchill, the undertaker enlisted by Winnie Trainor on behalf of the Thomson family, arrived at Canoe Lake by train. He brought with him a new steel casket. His task was to dig up the coffin in which Thomson was interred, transfer the body to the new casket and then see it safely on its way to Owen Sound via train. Despite an offer of help from Shannon Fraser, Churchill insisted on working alone in the dark by lamplight. Three hours later, the undertaker said he was done. This would have meant that in just 180 minutes, he had excavated four cubic metres of earth with nothing more than a shovel, opened the coffin, removed the body, placed it in the new coffin, soldered the second coffin shut and refilled the empty grave with earth—all by himself.

Ranger Robertson was highly skeptical of Churchill's claims, but with deep misgivings, he allowed the undertaker to board the train with the new coffin, which the porters at the train station said was suspiciously light. When he returned to the gravesite, Robinson found a shallow dent there and little other evidence of digging—Churchill could have simply dug up a small amount of earth and scattered it in the bushes to create the appearance of a grave that had been dug up and then filled in again.

Robinson had misgivings about the way the entire case had been handled. He thought that the bruise on Thomson's left temple could have just as easily been from a deliberate blow by a paddle as from an accidental capsizing. Furthermore, Thomson's paddle had never been found but should have floated ashore somewhere in the little lake; despite diligent searches by Robinson, no trace of Thomson's paddle could be found. There was also the hasty, slipshod manner in which the inquest was carried out—in fact, there had not really been an inquest. Then there was the fishing line wrapped neatly and deliberately 17 times around Thomson's left ankle. But unfortunately for Robinson, park superintendent Bartlett wanted the whole affair closed, as did the Thomson family—no further inquiries were welcome.

In the days following Thomson's death, speculation ran rampant that undertaker Churchill had not done any of the work he was paid for and that Thomson's body was lying not in Owen Sound where the family wished, but in the picturesque surroundings of Algonquin Park.

~

Interest in the Thomson mystery stayed strong, though. Through the 1920s, '30s and '40s, new articles and other short publications appeared every few years. Letters and correspond- ence were exchanged between interested parties and all the local players in the tragedy. Reminiscences were written down and recorded, and the evidence was sifted over in a haphazard series of revisitings and half-hearted inquiries.

And that was where things stood until the weekend before Thanksgiving 1956. That fateful weekend, a family court judge named William T. Little was staying at Canoe Lake. Little had been going there for years and had long been intrigued by all the speculation around Tom Thomson's death and final resting place. Along with three other friends, Little tramped up to the

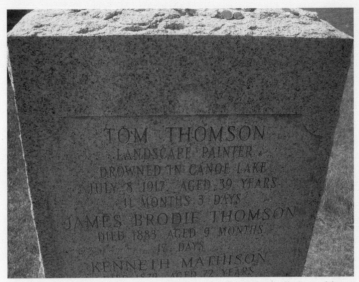

Tom Thomson grave marker in Leith, Ontario: But is he really buried here? The evidence suggests not.

~

park cemetery where Thomson's body was supposedly buried and simply started digging. They dug holes equal to two full graves without finding a thing, but on their third try, they unearthed a rotting wooden box with a skeleton inside it. The skull had what looked like a .22-calibre bullet hole in the left temple.

After getting help and notifying the authorities, Little's group submitted the bones for forensic examination. Although the evidence wildly contradicted any such conclusion, the Office of the Attorney General of Ontario supported its experts' contention that the bones were actually those of a 22-year-old male of Aboriginal ancestry. The small hole in the left temple, they said, had come from an operation called trephination, in which the skull of a living person is pierced to relieve pressure on the brain. The Thomson family again refused to allow the exhumation of the Owen Sound coffin to see if it contained Tom's body. Frustrated but having no other recourse, Judge Little and his cohorts returned the bones to Algonquin Park and buried them once more.

It seemed that the mystery of where Tom Thomson was actually buried might never be solved, that is, until the 2010 publication of Roy MacGregor's book, *Northern Light: The Enduring Mystery of Tom Thomson and the Woman Who Loved Him.* MacGregor, a prolific Canadian writer, had grown up in the area around Canoe Lake. Over the years, he had become acquainted (and conducted interviews) with many of the key players in the mystery or their surviving families. In his youth, he had even known the elderly Winnie Trainor, who lived as a spinster in a tiny apartment.

To solve the mystery of the skeleton in Algonquin Park, MacGregor employed considerable determination and ingenuity. Unable and unwilling to make another attempt to dig up the bones, he located previously unpublished photos of the skull, taken when it was unearthed in 1956. Next, he contacted the Toronto firm Archaeological Services Inc., a company that, among other things, specializes in reconstructing human remains. MacGregor gave them the photos of the skull as well as photos of Tom Thomson. After using every scientific tool available without, of course, having access to the actual skull, and submitting the materials to multiple forensic experts, Archaeological Services concluded that the odds were astronomically against the skull belonging to anyone *but* Tom Thomson. Moreover, the hole in the skull had likely been caused by a sharp blow from a pointed object as opposed to a bullet or even trephination.

But there was still one more step. Through Archaeological Services, MacGregor contacted renowned forensic artist Victoria Lywood, who is based in Montréal. Lywood's specialty is helping the police to create images of how unidentified human remains might have appeared when they were still part of a living person. MacGregor handed over the pictures of the skull, telling Lywood only that, according to Archaeological Services, it had likely belonged to a male of around 40, who was of European ancestry and who would have worn his straight, black hair parted on the left. Based on this information, Lywood began her reconstruction and, a few weeks later, produced a portrait that was undeniably Tom Thomson—right down to the strong bridge of his nose flowing naturally from the skull's nasal ridge.

~

Roy MacGregor's investigations had seemingly solved the mystery of Tom Thomson's final resting place, but there was still the question of the painter's actual demise. Here, MacGregor was no less exhaustive in his research. Since the 1970s, MacGregor had interviewed anyone who had known Tom Thomson or been a Canoe Lake regular during Thomson's years there. Although MacGregor's researches began too late to inter-view Winnie Trainor, who died in 1962 at the age of 77, his persistence and dedication were repaid with scores of interviews with other people who had been at Canoe Lake that fateful summer in 1917. His perseverance also put to rest a theory about Thomson's death that had been more or less the accepted version of events since the 1970s.

In 1970, William Little, the instigator of the 1956 dig, published his book, *The Tom Thomson Mystery*. It quickly became a bestseller, not least for its assertion that Tom Thomson had been murdered, possibly by Martin Blecher Jr., the man with whom he had argued the night before his death. Dr. Harry Ebbs, who had helped Little examine the remains, even postu-lated that Blecher had shot Thomson through the head as he was canoeing. But in 1977, Roy MacGregor tracked down someone who gave a different version of events.

Daphne Crombie and her husband had stayed at Canoe Lake during the time that Tom Thomson resided there. The Crombies were not present when the painter met his end, but they returned shortly afterward. During her time at Canoe Lake, Daphne had become friends with Annie Fraser. In fact, the two women appear as strolling figures in the foreground of Thomson's painting *Larry Dickson's Cabin*, Annie in a red coat and Daphne in blue. After the events of July 1917, Annie told Daphne a tale that seemed plausible and fit the known facts.

When Roy MacGregor interviewed Daphne in 1977, she told him how it had all happened.

Almost 60 years earlier, following Tom Thomson's death, Annie and Daphne had been out for a walk, much as they were when Thomson daubed their figures into his painting. But on this walk, Annie confessed to Daphne that one day she had been cleaning up Thomson's room when she came across a letter from Winnie Trainor. Annie, being a bit of a gossip, read the letter and discovered that it was an earnest entreaty for Thomson to buy a new suit since the two of them would *have* to get married because there was a baby on the way.

Shortly after this, there was a confrontation between Thomson and Annie's husband, Shannon. While there are many possible reasons for the fight, at different points in her life, Annie Fraser put forth two theories. The first was that Thomson, perhaps because he needed to buy the new suit for the wedding, demanded the immediate return of the $250 he had loaned Shannon Fraser earlier in the year to buy canoes. The second was the idea that Winnie's parents were angry about the pregnancy and had asked Shannon to "teach a lesson" to Thomson.

Either way, according to Annie, there was a scuffle between the two men. Shannon knocked the painter over close to the hearth and Thomson struck his head, possibly on one of the fire irons or some other sharp metal object, rendering him unconscious. In the heat of the moment, seeing the horrible wound, Shannon Fraser panicked and decided to dispose of the painter. According to Annie, she and her husband carried Thomson out to the canoe. Shannon wrapped the fishing line several times around the painter's ankle and tied the other end to a heavy weight. Then Shannon paddled out into the lake, towing Thomson behind the canoe, unconscious, submerged and drowning. Finally, under the cover of dark, Fraser cut loose his tragic and ghastly trawl, whereupon the now-lifeless Thomson settled to the bottom of the lake.

Winnie Trainor lived in Huntsville for the rest of her life and never married, nor as far as anyone could tell, was ever romantically involved with anyone. She was tight-lipped about her relationship with Thomson. In spite of all the help she had given the Thomson family when arranging for Tom's burial, the staid and proper Thomsons showed no interest in having anything to do with this woman who said that she and their son had been in love. Winnie is not known to have had any children, but, perhaps significantly, she did go away with her mother late in 1917 to spend the winter in Philadelphia, only returning to Huntsville around Easter 1918. Had she been away to have the child and give it up for adoption? Or simply to escape from the painful memories of Canoe Lake? These possibilities, of course, only raise another mystery, one to which we shall likely never have even an inkling of an answer—somewhere out there, does Tom Thomson have descendants?

Chapter Seventeen

The Disappearance of Ambrose Small

~

O n the snowy morning of December 2, 1919, a handful of people gathered in the boardroom of a lawyer's office at 65 Yonge Street in Toronto. They were there to complete the sale of a chain of vaudeville and movie theatres across Ontario. The owners, Ambrose J. Small and his wife, Theresa, were selling all of their theatres to the Trans-Canada Theatre Corporation. The sale price was $1.7 million—about $22 million in today's money.

Present were the Honorable W.J. Shaughnessy, legal representative of Trans-Canada Theatres; E.W.M. Flock, the Small's lawyer; and Theresa Small. Theresa was plump, dark-haired, rather dough-faced and well dressed. Although quiet and unassuming in person, she was known all over the city as a cultured, socially active woman who played the piano, spoke eight languages and collected art. In predominantly Protestant Toronto, she raised eyebrows by using her immense wealth to support numerous Catholic causes and initiatives. She was also an equal partner in the empire that she and her husband had built together.

The only person missing from the gathering was Ambrose Small, but this surprised no one—"Amby" was known for never being on time for anything. As the old saying goes, he'd probably be late to his own funeral and, in a manner of speaking, this would prove to be the case. Finally, at 10:45 AM, in a plume of blue cigar smoke, the ebullient, bright-eyed Small was ushered into the room. In contrast to the rather thickset figure of his wife, reticent, reserved and proper, Ambrose Small was slight, slender and outgoing. He was quick in his movements, and his vibrant blue eyes were constantly aglitter with either bonhomie or ambition. He was 55 years old, his brown hair just becoming flecked with grey. He wore his moustache in a luxuriant walrus-roll that completely hid his mouth. Small had been raised Protestant but did not practise his religion with much, if any, conviction, and certainly with nothing approaching his wife's devout Catholicism.

The lawyers, Shaughnessy and Flock, saw to it that the principals signed the documents of sale in all the right places. And then, from an inner pocket, Shaughnessy produced a cheque and handed it to Small—it was a down payment of $1 million. Mr. and Mrs. Small were reported to have beamed widely when they saw the money. Whatever their differences in demeanour and religion, the Smalls were united in their pursuit of wealth. Both Ambrose and Theresa endorsed the cheque. Ambrose handed it to his wife to take to the bank with a joking warning not to spend it all in one place. Flock said to her, "You will be the first person who carried a million dollar cheque up

Ambrose Small as he looked at the time of his disappearance

~

Yonge Street." Then the party broke up, with the Smalls and Flock making plans to meet for lunch in the tearoom of the nearby Grand Opera House.

Meanwhile, there were numerous details to see to regarding the smooth transition of ownership of the theatres. Not surprisingly, Flock and Small were late to their lunch date with Theresa at the Grand Opera House, but everyone was in a convivial mood anyway. After lunch, Theresa dragged a reluctant Ambrose up the street to the St. Vincent de Paul Children's Orphanage, where she was to present a Christmas donation of several thousand dollars. Gritting his teeth, Small went with her—he had no use for piety or charity, and almost everyone agreed that he was reluctant to part with money if it was not for business or pleasure.

Once the Smalls were done at the orphanage, the chauffeur drove Theresa home to their large house on Glen Road. Ambrose said he would be home around six o'clock for a celebratory dinner, but Theresa knew he would probably be late. Small's next appointment was a 4:00 PM meeting with Flock at the theatre that served as Small's headquarters, the Grand Opera House on Adelaide Street. The men planned to go over additional details of the sale, and then Flock would catch the six o'clock train to London.

Small was, of course, late to his meeting with Flock, showing up at about 4:30 PM. He told Flock that he had ordered a $9000 Cadillac for Theresa and a $10,000 necklace, though he did not specify who the necklace was for. The meeting wrapped up just after 5:30 PM. Flock hurriedly gathered his papers and made haste to catch his train. Small walked him to the door. Outside, Flock turned and waved to Small, who was now standing in the portico of a theatre he no longer owned. Small waved back, and Flock walked off through the swirling snow to Union Station.

He never saw Ambrose Small again.

～

Ambrose Small was born in 1863 in a log cabin in Adjala Township, 80 kilometres northwest of Toronto. In 1876, the family of three—father Daniel, mother Ellen and 13-year-old Ambrose—moved to Toronto. Daniel quickly found work as a shipper for Kormann Breweries and soon caught the eye of the owner, Ignatious Kormann, who promoted him to salesman, responsible for servicing all the hotels in Toronto. When a local theatre, the Grand Opera House, was rebuilt after a fire, Daniel Small was put in charge of the bar of the new adjoining hotel. Young Ambrose was put to work scrubbing glasses behind the bar.

Ambrose was enterprising and ambitious. He quickly graduated from managing the bar and running a gambling room in the back, to being the booking manager of the adjacent Grand Opera House. He had an instinct for profit, too, signing a string of lurid and lucrative melodramas that were the blockbusters of their day. During this time, he also became cozy with the Ontario racing commissioner, Thomas Flynn, and is thought to have won thousands of dollars on horse races based on inside information supplied by Flynn. In 1892, at the age of 29, Small was a mover and shaker on the rise, holding mortgages on two Toronto theatres and deeply involved in the city's gambling scene. Easy access to chorus girls had also given him a reputation as a womanizer who enjoyed frequent trysts with an ever-changing kick line of showgirl beauties. In short, he worked hard and played hard.

Ambrose's mother, Ellen, had died in 1884. A year later, Small's 41-year-old father, Daniel, married his boss' 19-year-old daughter, Josephine Kormann. The Kormann family recognized in Ambrose an ambitious, talented young man who was bent on being successful and was already acquiring the beginnings of a fortune that might one day rival their own. As the 19th century gave way to the 20th, Ambrose had starting sharing walks with the Kormann's youngest daughter, Theresa, and they married in 1902. Some said it was for love, others said it was for money. More than a few must have marvelled at Ambrose being simultaneously stepson *and* brother-in-law to Daniel's wife, Josephine, just as he was now both half-brother *and* uncle to their two children.

~

In 1904, little more than two years after they were married, Ambrose and Theresa could scarcely believe their luck when the Grand Opera House, which they now owned, was left undamaged by a massive fire that destroyed most of downtown Toronto. Even though the theatre had been spared, the close call set the Smalls to thinking that perhaps it was time to diversify their holdings. They quickly hatched a scheme to begin buying up theatres throughout Ontario.

To manage this undertaking, they would need help. The man they hired was 27-year-old John Doughty, who would serve as secretary-manager of the new enterprise. Although Doughty's duties were first and foremost managing the business' paperwork, he quickly proved himself to be a shrewd numbers man who could see through falsely inflated reports of other theatres' worth.

Thanks to Doughty's sharp financial eye, the Smalls were able to purchase theatres in other Ontario cities, including London, Peterborough and Windsor. Doughty's ability to read between the lines gave him a sixth sense that tingled sharply when he thought theatre owners might be willing to accept an offer to buy that was lower than the purported worth of their holdings.

The wage Doughty earned was, of course, a pittance compared to the profits he helped his employers to reap. Soon he began to resent the Smalls' accrual of more and more money by dint of *his* hard work. Doughty and Ambrose Small never really got along, but Small continued to put a great amount of trust in Doughty, giving him access to the couple's safe-deposit boxes at various banks and largely delegating the day-to-day running of the empire to him. Small cared nothing for interpersonal conflict as long as his business was profitable, as indeed it was. The police later estimated that Ambrose and Theresa had reached their goal of being millionaires around 1910.

But even as the family fortune was humming merrily along, the marriage, predictably, was not. Ambrose and Theresa slept in separate rooms. Theresa became more and more involved with her religion, even going so far as to build a lavish shrine in the basement of their house. Ambrose, on the other hand, though he had been raised Protestant, appeared to have no use for *any* religion. He had also probably never stopped his womanizing ways, and now, having no marriage bed to speak of, he continued his trysts with a seemingly endless parade of bloomer-flashing doxies. There were also rumours that Theresa engaged in discreet extramarital affairs. This was the state of things when Ambrose Small disappeared in 1919.

∼

On the evening of December 2, Ambrose failed to show up at home for his celebratory dinner with Theresa. She appears to have become worried, and as the evening wore on, made energetic inquiries to see if he had turned up at any of the theatres or stopped at any of his regular haunts. Theresa later told detectives that, although she was worried at the beginning, she wasn't entirely surprised because she thought her husband might have gone on an impromptu bender with some of his gambling cronies. Such sprees sometimes involved travelling to Mexico or other ports of call where loose morals and free-flowing booze abounded. At any rate, as the days went by, she did *not* report his disappearance to the police.

Meanwhile, one of the very cronies with whom Small might have been celebrating—his old friend, Thomas Flynn— became concerned at his absence. Every day for two weeks, Flynn showed up at the Grand Opera House looking for Small. Finally, he'd had enough and went to the police on December 16, a full fortnight after Small had last been seen. Flynn tried to speak to Chief Inspector George Guthrie, but was passed down the line to Detective Austin Mitchell. When Flynn told his story, Mitchell said that Mrs. Small had not reported her husband missing and suggested that Ambrose had probably gone on some sort of extended debauch in another city. Small was quite well known at this time and had a reputation as a well-travelled gambler, so Detective Mitchell's suggestion was not as cavalier as it may seem in hindsight. The police did, however, visit Small's office at the Grand Opera House on December 16 and found the furniture there to be "disarranged," with a foot broken off one of the chairs.

That same day, Detective Mitchell interviewed Theresa Small at her home. He found her to be very worried but felt also that she was "withholding something." The next day, December 17, Mitchell returned with another detective, who was named Archibald, and Theresa confessed that she knew that her husband had a regular mistress named Clara Smith. She thought he might have run off with Clara but would probably return. Moreover, according to Detective Mitchell, "she believed that if she advertised his disappearance, should he return to her, he would be very much annoyed at her doing so." This, then, was why Theresa had delayed reporting her husband's disappearance to the police. Detective Mitchell returned on December 18 and 19, asking Mrs. Small to account for her movements on the day of the disappearance and later searching the house, but he found nothing incriminating.

Mitchell now began looking for James Doughty and must have been annoyed when he learned from James Cowan, manager of the Grand Opera House, that Doughty had been in Toronto and had visited Theresa Small on December 29.

Ambrose and Theresa Small's house as it looks today: Could Ambrose be
buried in the basement?

~

Mitchell discovered this on December 30 and immediately went
to the Smalls' house. There he learned that Theresa had left messages at the Grand Opera House and Doughty's home for him
to call her as soon as he was back in town since "she believed
there wasn't anybody who would know better where her husband was." When Mitchell asked why she had not reported this
to him, she replied, "I didn't know you wanted to see him or
whether you had seen him." Mitchell seems to have accepted all
of this at face value, even though it must have struck him as odd.

Ambrose Small's racing crony Thomas Flynn would have
none of it and started going to all the Toronto clubs where

Ambrose was a regular, but no one had seen him. Finally, after another two weeks had passed, Flynn went to the *Toronto Star* on January 2, 1920, exactly one month after Small had disappeared. The *Star* jumped on the story, and by that night, three reporters had been assigned to the case and a front-page story was being prepared for the next day's edition. The attention of the press meant that the police had to step up their game, but they would be scooped to the first real clue by the reporters at the *Toronto Star*—the paper broke the news that John Doughty had also disappeared.

~

It later emerged that John Doughty's services had been sold to the new owners of the Smalls' properties, Trans-Canada Theatres Limited, and he had been transferred to Montréal. Doughty showed up for work there on December 3, later travelling back to Toronto to visit his children (he was a widower), whom he had left in the care of his sister, Jeanie. After seeing his family—and visiting Theresa Small—on December 29, he told everyone that he was heading back to Montréal, and no one had seen him since.

Detective Mitchell soon discovered that on December 2, the day of Small's disappearance, John Doughty had appeared at the Smalls' bank and removed $100,000 worth of negotiable bonds from the Smalls' safe-deposit box. At the trial, it came out that Doughty had actually removed the bonds over three visits, the first on December 1, followed by two visits on December 2.

It also emerged that Doughty had approached numerous co-workers to go in with him on various schemes to steal large amounts of money from Small, ranging from $75,000 to $300,000. On these occasions, he called Ambrose a "damn rogue" and "a lousy, cheap bastard," and said he wanted to kill the "son of a bitch." Another time, he "spoke of being dissatisfied with his job, wanted to know if it was possible to kidnap a man…"

Incredible as it may seem, Detective Mitchell appears to have regarded the disappearances of Small and Doughty as either unrelated or connected only in as far as both men might have gone on a bender together. He did at least put out an all-points bulletin for Ambrose Small.

Mitchell's superior, Chief Inspector Guthrie, seems to have been unimpressed by his subordinate's reluctance to press Theresa Small for more answers. Guthrie thought it was suspicious that Theresa had not gone to the bank after Small's disappearance to see if he had withdrawn money from either their accounts or the safe-deposit boxes. Guthrie brought in a detective from the Ontario Provincial Police, Edward L. Hammond of the Criminal Investigation Branch. Hammond was no star investigator, having badly botched his most recent case by rather gullibly buying some of the fraudulent stocks he was supposed to be investigating. Guthrie also formed his own force of detectives that had nothing to do with either Mitchell or Hammond.

There were now three different task forces searching for any clue as to the whereabouts of Ambrose Small.

At this time, in Canada, a murder charge could not be laid unless a body was found and there was evidence of murder on the body, so the next step for the police was to try to locate the corpse of Ambrose Small. Mitchell followed every clue that came up—he dredged a stretch of the Lake Ontario shoreline; he had his men dig up a considerable portion of the Rosedale Ravine after a witness reported seeing a group of men burying something in the frozen ground on the night that Small disappeared; and he even requisitioned a steam shovel and had his men spend smelly weeks going through the city dump. Whenever an anonymous body turned up anywhere in southern Ontario, Mitchell was there. Alas, it was all to no avail— Ambrose Small had vanished.

Detectives Mitchell and Hammond were men of wildly different temperaments and dispositions. Mitchell was slow, methodical and perhaps overly deferential to the social status of Theresa Small. Hammond was opinionated, far-reaching in his conclusions and seems to have had a fairly "creative" memory as far as evidence was concerned.

Their final reports on the Small case were both marked "Secret and Confidential" when submitted to the Office of the Attorney General of Ontario. This was likely because Toronto, at that time, was still riven by tension between Protestants and Catholics. Hammond's allegations about the Catholic Theresa could have ignited a firestorm of sectarian turmoil.

Both Mitchell and Hammond agreed that James Doughty had almost certainly abducted and killed Ambrose Small, but Hammond went one giant step further, concluding that Small "was the victim of a cunningly and well-conceived plan in which Mrs. Theresa Small his wife was the prime mover, and furthermore, I believe was actually present when her husband was murdered...also that John Doughty her husband's secretary was one of the murderers too."

Luckily for history, we have Detective Mitchell's clearly written, point-by-point rebuttal to Hammond's outrageous claims. For instance, central to Hammond's case was the supposed testimony of James Cowan, manager of the Grand Opera House, that "he had caught John Doughty and Mrs. Small having sexual intercourse on more than one occasion." Mitchell, to whom Cowan had actually given his statement, countered that what Cowan said was "that he had caught Doughty having sexual intercourse with one of the *scrubwomen* in the basement of the Grand Opera House." [Author's italics] Mitchell also pointed out that if Mrs. Small and Doughty were lovers, it would have been odd for Theresa to post a $15,000 reward, as she subsequently did, for information leading to his arrest.

Hammond's tendency to irrationally misread the available evidence is perhaps best illustrated by his mangling of Theresa's statement to a witness, Mrs. Kelly. Hammond wrote that "Mrs. Small told Mrs. Kelly that her husband had been taken away in a car, and she was afraid he had met with an accident." With a tone of paranoid outrage, Hammond then wants to know why, if Mrs. Small was so concerned about her husband, she did not report this apparent abduction to the police? According to Hammond, what Theresa actually said to Mrs. Kelly was simply that, the last time she had seen her husband, "he had <u>gone out</u> in a motor car, <u>not</u> [been] <u>taken away in a motor car</u>."

In the end, it comes down to a question of which man one chooses to believe. Hammond's interpretation of the evidence is suspect at best, and his accuracy is certainly questionable. However, Hammond also asserted that Mitchell was determined to protect Mrs. Small and said this several times in front of different witnesses. There is even an affidavit, signed by one Burton Keyser, swearing that Mitchell offered him a $50,000 reward if Keyser could produce just one human bone that Mitchell would then say was Small's and close the case, which he was becoming sick of. Mitchell, of course, denied the allegations, and they do, indeed, seem out of character for him—but the thing about a mystery is that one simply never knows.

~

As the investigation progressed, the lurid revelations just kept coming. Small had constructed a secret room at the Grand Opera House, the existence of which was known to very few people and certainly not to Theresa. Breaking into the room, the police could have been forgiven for thinking they had stumbled upon a bordello. The walls were hung with luxurious draperies to dampen sound, and the floor was covered with an Oriental carpet. There was a nude painting on one wall and a large bed along the other. There was even a small bar with two used whisky glasses on it. But the room smelled stale and the whisky decanters were covered in dust—there were no papers or other clues there, just an opulent but abandoned love nest.

An elderly furnace man at the Grand, Thomas Shields, reported that he had seen John Doughty standing over Small in the furnace room with a shovel raised as though he was about to hit his employer over the head with it. Pressed as to why he had not reported this earlier, he replied that he was infirm and was worried that the attention might compromise his health. Shields further qualified his assertion by saying that he had only glimpsed the scene for a fraction of a second through the crack of the furnace-room door and then, frightened, he had hurried away, not really sure what he had seen. It wasn't exactly reliable testimony. A former theatre janitor named Fred Osborne reported that Doughty had often spoken of how he would like to murder Small and make off with this money.

It was a frustrating series of dead ends, red herrings and unverifiable statements.

~

The break in the case, when it finally came, was thanks to the Royal Canadian Mounted Police. The Mounties had sensibly blanketed North America and parts of Europe with "Wanted" notices showing John Doughty. They had also posted a reward for information leading to his apprehension. In September 1920, reports emerged from a lumber camp in Portland, Oregon, that a man named Charlie Cooper was a dead ringer for Doughty.

Detective Mitchell's superiors sent him to Oregon. After observing "Charlie Cooper," Mitchell simply marched up behind his quarry, clapped a hand on the man's shoulder and said, "Hello, Jack. How are you?"

The man wanted to know who Mitchell was. The detective identified himself, whereupon the suspect seemed to become dizzy and blurted out, "I'm Doughty. I'm the man you're looking for."

∼

Detective Mitchell returned to Toronto with John Doughty in custody. In the absence of a body or anything beyond purely circumstantial evidence, Doughty was initially charged with conspiracy to kidnap Ambrose Small, as well as the theft of the bonds. But because of the lack of any substantial evidence, the conspiracy charge was dropped, and Doughty only stood trial for the theft of the bonds.

Doughty seemed eager to co-operate with the police and took them to the house where his sister, Jeanie, lived with his children. After greeting his family, Doughty asked Jeanie, whom the detectives had already interviewed more than once, to fetch the package he had left with her for safekeeping. She went upstairs and returned shortly with a paper-wrapped package—the missing $100,000 in negotiable bonds.

The trial was quick but tumultuous. Although he never took the stand, Doughty had told police upon his arrest that Small had *given* him the bonds as a reward for his years of service. When Theresa Small took the stand, it was only for a few moments—much to the disappointment of the press—to contradict Doughty's assertion that Small had gifted him the bonds. "Amby wouldn't have given away 10 cents unless he was getting 20 cents back," she said.

~

In the end, John Doughty was convicted of the theft of the bonds and sentenced to five years in prison. But the fate of Ambrose Small remained a mystery, and the sensationalism surrounding his disappearance continued. Doughty served his five-year sentence and lived out the rest of his days running a service station in Toronto's East End. After years of legal wrangling, Theresa Small finally gained control of the $2 million estate and, upon her death in 1935, true to her word, she left the whole thing to various Catholic orders and charities. But because Theresa's will had to be probated, the whole case was again torn wide open. In 1936, 17 years after Small's disappearance, the Attorney General of Ontario launched a full-scale probe that, among other things, had Detective Mitchell dig up the floor of the Smalls' Glen Road home for the *second* time, desperately looking for any shred of concrete evidence concerning Ambrose's fate. Suspicion abounded that Theresa and Doughty had somehow been in on it together, though no conclusive evidence was ever brought forth to bolster this notion.

When the Grand Opera House was demolished in May 1944, Detective Mitchell was there to take one last look around. Years earlier, he had dug up the floor of the furnace room to look for the body of Ambrose Small. Now, separate from the vast crowd of onlookers (the case had never really died out of the public's imagination), he squinted through the rubble but only saw what he had seen before—nothing. All that rose out of the gritty dust of the theatre's ruins were the same old questions.

Chapter Eighteen

The Disappearance of Rocco Perri

~

Rocco Perri was a self-made criminal and an immensely successful one. Born into a poor family in Italy's Calabria region in 1887, he and his family moved to Canada in 1908. Rocco tried a number of honest but poorly paid jobs, even working for a short time in a quarry near Parry Sound. He took his first step toward criminal greatness when he knocked on the door of a new rooming house in Toronto where he hoped to lodge. The woman of the house, Bessie Starkman, opened the door. She was petite, pretty, blue-eyed and married with two children. She and Rocco fell for each other at first sight, and after a few months of torrid infidelity, she abandoned her family and moved to St. Catharines with Rocco. Although they didn't know it at the time, the two of them had just embarked on what would be a wildly successful life of crime.

By 1916, Rocco and Bessie had saved a bit of money by working mostly honest jobs, and they moved to Hamilton. This was where things kicked into high gear. Ontario declared prohibition in 1916—a person could no longer have an honest drink at the end of the day. Rocco and Bessie opened a small grocery store and started making their own liquor, using potato peelings for the mash that would eventually yield potent liquor that the pair sold for half a buck a shot.

Needless to say, in a thirsty, hardworking town like Hamilton, Rocco and Bessie's grocery store did *very* well. Pumping out over 750 litres of potato whisky every week, the couple was quick to see that theirs could be but the first branch of a vast bootlegging franchise. In short order, the friendly and persuasive Rocco had enlisted a web of family and friends to run their own "grocery stores," all funnelling their profits into his and Bessie's ever-deepening pockets. The whole thing was, of course, highly illegal. However, after a hard day spent trying to enforce futile prohibition laws, Hamilton's judges, politicians and police officers often wanted nothing more than a good, stiff drink. And so it was that Rocco and Bessie found themselves in a friendly atmosphere of overlooked transgressions and a highly profitable absence of competition.

After joining forces with booze smugglers in the U.S., including the infamous Lucky Luciano, Rocco consolidated his position as eastern Canada's most powerful rum-runner. As the middle years of the 1920s arrived, Rocco and Bessie had become local celebrities—they dressed in the finest clothes and bought a big, fancy house. Bessie wore expensive jewels, and the couple entertained generously and often, hobnobbing with the city's worthies. In 1923, though, Rocco would sow the first seeds of his own destruction.

Two minor bootleggers named Joe Boytovich and Fred Genessee arrived in Hamilton and set about manufacturing inferior whisky at cut-rate prices. Rocco's response was to have a couple of his henchman kidnap the pair in the middle of a snowstorm and transport them out of town to a warehouse. A few hours later, Rocco arrived at the warehouse and stomped on Boytovich's chest until he passed out. Switching to his fists, he then pummelled Genessee's face into a bloody pulp. After this, Perri's henchmen waited until dark, then took the bound men to separate locations and shot them dead.

With these cold-blooded murders, Rocco's easy relations with the police came to an end. Hamilton's lawmakers became focused on prosecuting both Rocco and Bessie, but as to the murders, no evidence could be found against the couple. By this time, though, the government was determined—if they couldn't arrest Rocco and Bessie for murder, they would get them for bootlegging.

In 1927, prohibition was repealed in Ontario, but those who had smuggled liquor prior to that were still liable to prosecution. That was why, in 1928, the Crown launched a Royal Commission to look into Bessie and Rocco's bootlegging activities. Rocco protested that he was a simple pasta salesman who had made his fortune by working hard and selling his pasta door to door. The Crown was of the opinion that earning $780,000 in one year meant selling an awful lot of noodles. And that was just Rocco's income—they soon discovered an additional *eight* bank accounts in Bessie's name, further learning that she had deposited $900,000 into one of them *all at once*. As part of a plea bargain that saw the charges against Bessie dropped, Rocco pleaded guilty to perjury and spent six months in a reformatory.

This left Bessie to run the empire, which she did with felonious aplomb. Having always been the financial brains in the family enterprise, Bessie seamlessly took over as the leader of the Calabrian mob. She continued in her role as chief money launderer and now took the mob into the profitable new territory of narcotics, peddling $250,000 worth of marijuana, opium and cocaine per week. Once, during an RCMP raid on a known drug house in Toronto, Bessie showed up carrying hundreds of dollars in cash, but since this in itself was not illegal, the police had to release her. When he got out of prison, Rocco simply left Bessie in charge, much to the chagrin of other crime bosses who likely resented a woman being in command—especially one who refused to share the Hamilton mob's ill-gotten gains with chapters in other cities and who was frequently arrogant and high-handed.

On August 13, 1930, at 11:00 PM, the Perris were drunkenly returning to their house from a party when two shotgun blasts rang out and Bessie fell to the ground, mortally wounded. Such was her local popularity that an unruly crowd of thousands attended her funeral a few days later and tried to push through the police barriers. Rocco was left a broken man. He became involved with another strong woman, Annie Newman, but the steady decline in Rocco's criminal fortunes showed what a key player Bessie had been in the Calabrian mob's Hamilton success. In 1933, U.S. prohibition was finally repealed, radically reducing Perri's income potential. As the 1930s wore on, Rocco's influence began to wane as, seemingly, did his drive.

In 1938, there were two separate bomb attempts on his life, but he escaped both times, albeit once only narrowly. Even then, the RCMP was still determined to get their man, and with Canada's entry into World War II, they finally had the necessary tools at their disposal. Under the War Measures Act, Canadians born in any one of the Axis powers—Germany, Italy or Japan—could be rounded up and sent to detention camps for fear that they were in cahoots with their enemy countrymen. In 1940, the Mounties swooped in, grabbed the Italian-born Perri and packed the now-greying mobster off to a detention camp, where he stayed until his release in 1943.

Now truly a shadow of his former self, Perri worked odd jobs in Toronto before mustering his resolve to make one last crooked go of it in Hamilton. Alas, Rocco Perri was now more likely to be laughed at than feared—he was an aging relic from another time, unable to see that organized crime had changed and that a fresh crop of pimps, killers and bosses had taken over. All the more puzzling then, that on April 23, 1943, after supper at his cousin's house just north of Hamilton, Rocco Perri walked out the door to get some air and was never seen again.

Was his disappearance the result of some old gangland score being settled? Was he killed by disgruntled members of his own mob? Old rivals from another? Vigilantes settling his debt to the public? Young hoods simply tired of seeing him around? Did they make him suffer or was it quick? What did they do with the body?

The mystery of Rocco Perri's disappearance may have once had a solution, but the passage of time has surely carried off anyone who knew the answers.

Chapter Nineteen

The Kenora Bomber

~

Some mysteries involve unknown creatures such as Bigfoot, the Loch Ness Monster or the Jersey Devil, whereas others involve mysterious phenomena. Was a particular location really haunted? How can we explain UFO abduction experiences? However, we are about to explore yet another type of mystery, one in which all of the facts are well documented, but the identity of the key player remains unknown. Mysteries that ask *who*, rather than *what,* are particularly tantalizing, perhaps because *who* is the question we ask ourselves whenever we meet someone for the first time or go on a first date. Who *is* this person? What makes this person tick? How have the events of this person's life unfolded to bring them to this moment?

~

For the employees of the Canadian Imperial Bank of Commerce (CIBC) in Kenora, the afternoon of May 10, 1973, unfolded like any other. Familiar faces came into the bank, made their transactions and left. Eyes began to dart down to wristwatches as the closing hour of three o'clock approached.

It seemed to be another routine end to another routine day. But not quite. In fact, not at all.

At about five minutes to three, a man entered the bank wearing a nylon stocking pulled over his head as mask. In the words of one witness, "he had a pink shirt on, he looked like an old-time frontiersman." The man walked calmly into the office of bank manager Al Reid and told Reid that he carried with him in a duffle bag six sticks of dynamite and a tin of gasoline. He then produced a .32-calibre automatic pistol and, according to some accounts, a rifle as well. Very soft-spoken at all times, the man—as far as anyone was able to tell through the stocking— was in his fifties and seemed to have a reddish beard. His first demand to Al Reid was a simple, if threatening one.

"He said he would burn the place down if I didn't clear people out," Reid later told reporters. Wanting to avoid blood-shed, not to mention the possible incineration of his bank, Reid instructed his employees to leave, and then, at the urging of the robber himself, phoned the police just before three o'clock. Kenora's police chief, C.W. Engstrom, took Reid's call "to the effect that there was a man in his office who wanted some money. He was armed and dangerous and we were to use caution."

Meanwhile, the bank employees filed out. Now Al Reid and the bank robber were alone in the building. Just seven min-utes had passed since the man had walked through the doors.

The police soon arrived and entered the bank, but the masked thief ordered them out, and they complied. Inside, the robber started stuffing money into satchels and knapsacks. It was later estimated that he had bagged about $100,000 in all.

During this time, Chief Engstrom had not been idle. He called in reinforcements from the RCMP, OPP and even additional police from nearby Falcon Lake. This combined force cordoned off the bank to keep spectators out of the way—eventually 1000 onlookers would converge on the street to watch the drama play out. Officials also set up a series of roadblocks to control traffic in and out of town. Presently, Chief Engstrom received another call. It was Al Reid again, delivering the robber's demands. "He requested a pickup truck and a driver be stationed in front of the bank," said Engstrom, who set about complying with the robber's request.

Meanwhile, an enterprising radio reporter named Jack Allen, who worked at CHWO in far off Oakville, near Toronto, had heard about the holdup. He picked up the phone and placed a call to the bank. Al Reid answered:

Reid: *We're tied up right now. Can you call back a little later?*

Allen: *Are you with the police?*

Reid: *No, I'm the manager of the bank.*

Allen: *Is the guy still holding you hostage?*

Reid: *Yeah.*

Allen: *Well, can I speak with him?*

Reid: *You wanta talk to him?*

Allen: *Sure.*

[A pause]

Reid: *He won't talk.*

Allen: *How does it look?*

Reid: *He's got everything. He's looking for another bag. He
didn't bring enough bags with him to put all the
money in here. He's looking for another bag.*

A short exchange followed as Allen asked what kind of
gun the man had and confirmed that the bank manager and the
bank robber were the only ones in the building. And then:

Allen: *How does the guy expect to get out of there?*

Reid: *He's got a satchel in front of him here with six sticks
of dynamite in it and a deadman's switch in
his teeth.*

A "deadman's switch" is any sort of control that takes
effect when the operator *releases* pressure, presumably because of
loss of consciousness or death, hence the name. Normally, such
a switch is used as a safety feature. For example, some trains
have a foot pedal that must always be depressed in a "middle"
position; if the operator slumps forward, fully depressing the
pedal, or removes the pressure of his or her foot altogether,
the train will decelerate.

The deadman's switch used by the Kenora bank robber was, according to witnesses, a spring-loaded clothespin, the prongs of which were fitted with conductive metal leads attached to a battery or other detonator. The robber clamped the ends of the clothespin between his teeth in an "open" position, preventing the prongs from touching one another. In the event that the robber relaxed his jaw, the spring's tension would be released and the ends of the clothespin would touch, completing the electrical circuit and detonating the bomb. It is probably safe to assume that this was why the bank robber didn't want to talk to reporter Jack Allen—he already had the deadman's switch between his teeth.

There was another short exchange in which Allen asked Reid if the pickup truck demanded by the bank robber had arrived yet (it hadn't), and then:

Allen: *Does he appear to be very angry with you?*

Reid: *No. He just wants all the money he can get and he's taking off.*

Allen: *So you don't seem very frightened.*

Reid: *Well, I wouldn't say that.*

The phone call ended there, possibly because the getaway pickup truck ordered by the robber had arrived. Outside the bank, the police had been working fast. A 29-year-old, off-duty officer, Don Milliard, a father of two, volunteered to be the robber's driver. It was probably some time after 3:30 PM when Constable Milliard, in plain clothes, pulled up in the getaway vehicle that the robber had requested. It had been agreed that Milliard would be the robber's hostage, in exchange for the release of Al Reid.

Milliard went into the bank and told the robber, "I'm just a town employee." He said the man in the stocking mask seemed to relax a bit upon hearing this. The robber searched Milliard for weapons and, finding none, showed Milliard that he had now strapped the knapsack containing the dynamite to his chest. Two wires were plainly visible running from the explosives girdling the robber's stomach to the clothespin in his mouth. Outside the bank, police had done their best to clear the area, but the huge crowd had formed a massive human perimeter surrounding the scene, with people craning their necks over one another's shoulders to get a glimpse of the action. Chief Engstrom had also positioned at least one sniper, Sergeant Ron Letain, about 24 metres away, armed with a .308-calibre rifle.

Inside, the robber got Constable Milliard to carry the money, now stuffed into a cylindrical duffle bag about 120 centimetres long and 45 centimetres in diameter. Milliard hefted the bag over his left shoulder, where it hung like giant, droopy (and very expensive) sausage. Milliard turned and motioned for Reid to move farther into the building's interior. Then he and the bank robber began to exit the building with Milliard in the lead. As they emerged from the front doors, Milliard saw the robber reach down into one of his duffle bags and wind something three times with a sort of ratcheting sound.

"At that instant, I did not want to get into the truck," said Constable Milliard. "I was hoping someone would take action. That action by the robber scared me. I don't think I could have gotten into that truck."

In the grainy newspaper photos that chronicle the robbery, we first see Constable Milliard in the lead, the huge duffle bag slung over one shoulder. Two paces behind him is the robber, his head a dark blob under the stocking, but apparently also wearing a hat and looking rather portly because of the explosive duffle bag wired to his chest. In the next photo, we see Milliard in the foreground bent over slightly as if to put the money in the pickup truck. The robber stands motionless at the curb between two parked cars, now about two metres away from Milliard and the pickup truck. Just an instant after this, Milliard threw himself to the ground, presumably still holding the duffle bag stuffed with cash.

From his vantage point, sharpshooter Ron Letain had watched the two men come out of the bank. He could see that the robber still carried the .32-calibre automatic pistol. Letain would later testify, "I realized that if I were to shoot, it would be a fatal shot," presumably referring to the deadman's switch. "If not, the robber might use the revolver he was carrying to shoot Constable Milliard."

Letain had not been given specific orders to shoot, nor could he communicate with any of the other police officers in the area, but he made his decision. He squinted through his rifle's telescopic sight, took aim and fired.

John Berry, a reporter with radio station CJRL in Kenora, was covering the robbery from across the street when Milliard and the robber came out of the bank. His eyewitness account picks up just after Sergeant Letain has fired:

> *God in hell a bomb's gone off. A bomb's gone off. He's…my God…everything has gone crazy…What's going on? The smoke, the smoke. The bomb's gone off. There's smoke everywhere and money all over the street. A policeman has been shot. Men are running, two cars are completely heavily damaged, the entire front of the Canadian Imperial Bank of Commerce has just exploded. A helicopter is flying over top now…Windows have been blown out literally all over the place. There is debris…there is pieces of clothing and blood…*

Constable Milliard had not been shot as Berry thought, but the explosion had flung him seven and half metres away, where he landed in a broken heap on the ground. Milliard would survive but with significant injuries that were still causing him considerable pain when he testified a month later at the coroner's inquest. The duffle bag had probably saved his life by absorbing some of the explosion's force, tearing open and scattering its contents, which settled like a softly fluttering rain on the chaotic scene that followed the blast.

The bank robber's body was completely disintegrated by the explosion except for one of his hands, which was later retrieved by police and fingerprinted, but to no avail—the prints had no match in the police records of known offenders. Windows up and down the street were shattered. One onlooker who was standing more than 60 metres from the blast site suffered, of all things, a knife wound to the shoulder. Police later surmised that the knife had been on the robber's person and became a projectile when the bomb detonated. Two police officers and 10 bystanders were injured in the blast, but aside from the robber, there were no fatalities.

At the coroner's inquest a month later, the four-man, one-woman jury concluded that Sergeant Letain had been entirely justified in firing at the robber on his own initiative. They were unable to determine the severity of the (presumed) rifle wound and attributed the suspect's death to the detonation of his own bomb. Whether Sergeant Letain actually hit the robber and, if so, how severely the man was wounded, has remained open to debate. Witnesses at the scene said that they observed the police fire one or two shots, after which the robber blew himself up—whether he did so deliberately or involuntarily will never be known. This writer's opinion is that a police sharpshooter can probably be relied upon to hit his target. Either way, the coroner's jury also recommended that Constable Milliard be commended for actions "beyond the normal call of duty."

In September 1974, both Sargeant Letain and Constable Milliard were recognized with the Canadian Banks' Law Enforcement Award for officers who combat crimes against banks. Milliard also received $7300 in compensation for his injuries and eventually switched careers to join the fire department.

And what of the mysterious, soft-spoken, red-bearded bank robber? Aside from the fruitless attempt at fingerprint identification, all that police could learn was that he had been registered at a local hotel under a fictitious name and address, indicating that he was probably from out of town. In 2003, police thought they had identified the robber by extracting DNA from hair samples found at the scene of the explosion. But much to their chagrin, the man to whom the hair belonged was alive and well and living in France. Originally from Germany, the man had fallen on tough times in Canada, abandoned his leased truck in Winnipeg in 1973 and flown home to Europe.

Many questions remain unanswered. Who was the bank robber? And what could have driven him to such desperate lengths? His age—he seemed to be in his fifties, but was described by one newspaper as "elderly"—and his soft-spoken demeanour suggest that he could very well have been committing the robbery for some specific purpose. Did he have an ailing wife, child or even grandchild? Could he have been recently divorced and in need of money for alimony or to run away and start over? Did he have a farm or other property threatened by imminent foreclosure? Or was he simply tired of scrabbling along at some kind of dead-end life? He clearly wanted the money, but he was also fully prepared to die. What was at stake? His future? The life of another? An escape from a daily absence of hope that he could no longer bear?

We shall probably never know, but we can always continue to ask, "Who was this person?"

Chapter Twenty
The Telltale Mummy

~

I t was the evening of July 24, 2007. Thirty-seven-year-old renovator Bob Kinghorn was on his ladder on the second floor of an old house on Kintyre Avenue in East Toronto. When the house was built decades earlier, the ceiling of the second floor was finished in lath and plaster—narrow strips of wood covered in a hard plaster and mixed with horse hair for added strength. Above the room where Kinghorn was working was the attic. It was separated from the level below by a space between the attic floorboards and the laths that made up the ceiling of the second floor. This was the cavity that Bob Kinghorn was now rooting around in, hunting for electrical wires.

Peering up from the top of his stepladder through a gap in the lath, Kinghorn noticed a small cloth bundle tied up with string. It appeared to be quite old. Whoever had hidden it had probably done so from above—after all, prying up an attic floorboard is less conspicuous than getting on a ladder, then tearing out and replacing a chunk of overhead lath and plaster. Kinghorn dropped the package onto the floor, then climbed down from his ladder to investigate.

He could already smell an unpleasant odour of decay, later saying, "It smelled dead," and, "If you've smelled death, you know what it smells like." He cut the string that bound the cloth, which was later revealed to be a comforter, and it fell away to reveal the inner lining—an ancient page from Toronto's defunct newspaper, the *Mail and Empire*, dated September 15, 1925. At this point Kinghorn assumed he'd found the remains of a cat or a small dog, perhaps a beloved pet wrapped up and preserved by a grieving child more than 80 years earlier.

But when he tore open the old newspaper, Kinghorn was horrified to see that the package contained a tiny human, curled up in the fetal position—a mummified baby. "I counted the little fingers and toes," he said. "No! No! No! I got mad, threw off my headgear, kicked something and bounced out of the house. My first thought was murder. I thought, how could you do that? You sons of bitches!"

An autopsy was duly performed on "Baby Kintyre." Jim Cairns, Ontario's deputy chief coroner, was able to provide additional details that simultaneously eased minds, expanded the mystery and deepened the overall sense of sadness that affected anyone connected to the case. The body was that of a baby boy, said Cairns, and about 80 years old, a conclusion that was supported by the 1925 date of the newspaper page in which Baby Kintyre had been wrapped. An examination of the air sacs in the baby's lungs suggested that he had been born alive but died shortly afterward. There was no evidence of broken bones, stab marks or other injuries. No cause of death could be determined.

There were facts but no answers.

~

At first, it seemed futile to try to track down clues to an 80-year-old mystery—surely everyone involved was dead by now. But with the help of tips from the public, persistent reporters soon located 92-year-old Rita Rich, who was living in western New York State. Although Rita couldn't really provide any answers, she was lucid, her mind was sharp and her memories of those long-ago years were detailed. The story that Rita Rich recounted set the mystery of Baby Kintyre against the backdrop of everyday life in a busy family home bursting with the stories of the lives that had filled it so many years ago—passions, indiscretions and abiding love.

~

From 1919 to 1941, the house on Kintyre Avenue was owned by a postal clerk named Wesley Russell and his wife, Della, whose maiden name was Rutter. Della's brother, Charles Rutter, a barber and widower, lived in the house as well, along with his little daughter, Rita (who would later take her husband's family name of Rich). Rita's mother had died in the Spanish flu epidemic of 1918, and her father had never remarried or even dated. Indeed, so dedicated was he to the memory of his wife and the happiness of his daughter that every year, on

Rita's birthday, Charles would open a trunk of his late wife's belongings and give his daughter a piece of jewellery or other personal article, saying it was a gift from her mother. In 1925, Rita's room, the very attic beneath which Baby Kintyre would be found, was painted in cheery yellow and royal blue, with light streaming in through the front window and bouncing off the steeply sloped ceiling. Charles had also set up a little altar in the corner so Rita could say her prayers to her mother at night. The notion that her father was in any way involved with the baby hidden at her feet seemed rather unlikely.

Then there was the boarder, George Turner, who was in his twenties. Newly arrived from Ottawa, Turner had been befriended by Charles Rutter when he sat down in his barber chair for a haircut. Turner would board in the house for 10 years. He was someone who might at least be in a position to father a child who would be deemed unwanted. But Rita insisted that this would be unlikely behaviour for the gentle and compassionate man who became like a big brother to her. Whenever Rita walked north from Kintyre Avenue to catch the Dundas streetcar, Turner would go with her and be waiting at the stop for her when she was headed home again. If Turner had gotten a woman pregnant, Rita insisted, "He would have married her for sure. I mean, he was very much a gentleman."

Then there were Rita's aunt and uncle, Della and Wesley, the owners of the house. In the 1920s, while she was living on Kintyre Avenue, Rita remembered her Uncle Wesley as being a "second father." He was handy around the house, refinishing the basement as a den and diligently repainting the outside of the house every two years. He enjoyed making "homebrew," but Rita couldn't remember ever seeing him drunk. Della, Wesley's wife, had always been sad that she could not have children because of a childhood fall from a horse—one of her great desires in life was to be a mother, so it is difficult to imagine that, if by some miracle she had become pregnant, she would have hidden her pregnancy or the birth of a child.

However, in the 1930s, when Rita was in her teens and long after Baby Kintyre had been hidden under the attic floorboards, it emerged that Wesley had been having an affair with a younger woman. Della suffered a complete mental breakdown and tried to throw herself off the roof of the house. It remains unclear whether her husband's infidelity contributed to Della's mental illness or whether her mental illness may have been a contributing factor to Wesley's infidelity—or both. Either way, Della was packed off to an asylum and Wesley's new lover moved in. Rita moved out shortly afterward because she no longer felt comfortable living there.

Although later than the coroner's estimate (and the date of the newspaper) by 10 years, Wesley's situation does seem to be one that might have produced a possibly unwanted or unsuccessful pregnancy. One can't help but wonder if, unlikely as it may seem, perhaps the coroner's estimate of the baby's age was off by 10 years and that Wesley or his new lover, in some moment of unexplained panic, grabbed a 10-year-old sheet of newspaper that was perhaps serving as the lining of a drawer or closet and wrapped Baby Kintyre in his improvised shroud. It is a possibility, though an unlikely one, that still raises more questions than it answers.

However, the cast of characters in the Kintyre Avenue house is not exhausted yet—there was one more person, Della's younger sister, Alla Mae Rutter. Rita remembers Alla Mae as a beautiful, glamorous, blue-eyed blonde, 32 years old in 1925 and divorced. In contrast to the dowdy Della, Alla Mae wore black satin, dated bandleaders and carried around a poodle named Teddy. When she married, Alla Mae moved to New York to live with her husband. Their short-lived union ended when he returned from fighting in World War I in 1918, but during the years he was away, Alla Mae had soaked up the life of a socialite, doing embroidery for department stores by day and dating some of the best-known bandleaders of the era by night. She visited her family in Toronto more than once, and it was a memorable occasion for Rita when one of Alla Mae's New York bandleader beaux happened to be in Toronto at the same time and picked her up in his car at the door of the house.

Alla Mae Rutter is the strongest candidate for the mother of Baby Kintyre. Her glamour-girl lifestyle meant that she could very well have gotten pregnant. Her status as a divorcée would have lent an air of scandal to her life, but combined with the social mores of the times, having a child out of wedlock would have incurred crushing social stigma. It is also quite possible that she did not want to be a mother. And what better way for a young woman to rid herself of an unwanted child than to travel to another city, have and dispose of the baby there, and then return to New York? There are, of course, puzzling problems with this theory as well. Rita remembers that during one of Alla Mae's visits to the house, she was moving some furniture when Della chided her saying, "Don't do that or you will lose this baby." Rita further remembered, "It was as if Alla Mae didn't want the baby." Rita admits, however, that she is unsure of this memory.

Home to a mystery: Framed between the telephone pole and the tree is the house where the body of Baby Kintyre lay for 80 years.

"I would like to think it was so," she said, "then I would know she was the mother, but I don't know; it was so vague."

Assuming that Alla Mae was the baby's mother raises other questions. If Della knew that Alla Mae was pregnant, how would it have been possible and why would it have been necessary for Alla Mae to conceal the birth from everyone in the house? Was Della complicit in hiding the tiny body of her nephew? Unable to have a proper funeral, was hiding him under the floorboards perhaps deemed a more Christian thing to do than discarding him in the nearby Don River? And, most puzzlingly, how did Baby Kintyre die?

～

Because there are no answers, we are left to make choices and do the best we can. Rita Rich remembered the years on Kintyre Avenue as well as she could. The coroner assessed the facts to the best of his ability. Somewhere, near the beginning of the last century, a desperate, possibly frightened and aggrieved parent did what probably seemed like the best he or she could do in the circumstances. And Bob Kinghorn, the renovator who found Baby Kintyre, did the best he could as well—he set up a trust fund for Baby Kintyre to be peacefully buried in Toronto's Elgin Mills Cemetery, so the child could rest beneath grass, flowers and trees.

CRYPTIC CREATURES

Chapter Twenty-one

Early Lake Monsters

~

anada has a long tradition of lake monsters, mysterious freshwater creatures lurking just beneath the surface, perhaps even brushing past the blade of your canoe paddle. With upward of 30,000 lakes having an area of at least three square kilometres (many more if you count smaller lakes), it is hardly surprising that, since time immemorial, Canada's inhabitants have reported strange sights on these inland water bodies. Before the arrival of Europeans, First Nations all across North America knew that, like rocks, trees and air, the watery depths were animated by spirits. Tales of hitherto unknown marine animals lurking in lakes were particularly numerous in Québec, with European settlers eagerly embracing and likely embellishing the accounts passed on by First Nations peoples.

Québec may have the highest population of lake monsters, but British Columbia is home to the most famous by far—Ogopogo, said to lurk beneath the placid waters of Lake Okanagan. Between these poles of east and west, however, the other provinces boast their fair share of sightings. Manipogo is a serpentine beast that traditionally inhabits the waters of Lake Manitoba. Ontario's most famous "loch lurker" is probably Igopogo (now lamely renamed Kempenfelt Kelly), often spotted along the shores of Lake Simcoe. We shall certainly give Igopogo its due in the pages that lie ahead, but first, a brief overview of other creatures espied surfacing from the murky depths of Ontario's lakes.

Main Duck Island, 1840

At the easterly end of Lake Ontario lies a pocket of islands known collectively as "The Ducks." Almost 20 kilometres from the mainland, the largest of these is Main Duck Island. According to local legend, the island is home to buried treasure, but that is not our concern. Scattered in an around The Ducks lies a treacherous minefield of shoals and boulders, some partially submerged, others half-protruding from the water. One day in 1840, a schooner was sailing past Main Duck Island when the captain observed a shoal that did not appear on any of his charts. We have to assume that the captain did not spot the "shoal" until his ship was upon it, for the schooner sailed over top of the thing, whereupon the object was observed to be a peacefully slumbering "sea" serpent. The creature was about 15 metres long, covered in brown scales, with a head like a dragon and a tail resembling the barbed head of a harpoon. On being run over by the schooner, the unfortunate serpent was cleft asunder, and the startled captain watched as the two severed halves swam off in opposite directions. Readers are left to judge for themselves the truthfulness of this account, as well as the competence and sobriety of the captain.

Tobermory, 1873

The Bruce Peninsula pushes northward into the waters of Lake Huron, its 100-kilometre length separating Georgian Bay from the rest of the lake. Located at its northernmost tip is the community of Tobermory. Not far from these shores lies the prosaically named Bear's Rump Island, and it was there, in 1873, that the lake monster since known as "Tobey" was first sighted. In an account later published in the *Owen Sound Courier Herald*, Captain Campbell MacGregor reported his hair-raising encounter with an aquatic beast that he estimated to be nearly as large as his 21-metre-long fishing schooner *Talisman*.

Captain MacGregor said that the creature was "blackish in colour, having a body like a giant seal, with flippers and a neck as long as its body. And them eyes! I'll never forget it staring at me with coal black eyes the size of dinner plates."

Four years later, in 1877, the schooner *Intrepid* faltered into Tobermory's Little Tub Harbour. Badly damaged below its waterline, the ship was intrepid no more and eventually sank within the harbour's confines. This time there were multiple witnesses, passengers who said that the *Intrepid* had collided with something they had presumed to be a log, but which "raised its ugly head, looked at us and then swam away." In 1948,

Tobey appeared again, swimming along beside the cruise ship *City of Detroit* for several hundred metres. The *City of Detroit*'s amazed passengers and crew described a creature 18 metres long with "a snake-like body and horned head."

Skeptics uncharitably suggest that the bottom of the lake is permeated with gases that are mistaken for Tobey when they bubble to the surface. Indeed, the submarine geology of the Tobermory region is remarkable, being a series of underwater cliffs, caverns and ridges that are an extension of the Niagara Escarpment. Believers, on the other hand, posit that these sub-aqueous caves and grottoes are the home of the monster itself, not merely pockets of gas.

As tempting as it is for skeptics to ascribe Tobey sight-ings to a lot of gas, others suggest that the creature could be a relict species left behind when the glacial waters of the last ice age receded, cutting off the Great Lakes from the oceans. This theory is not entirely without merit—the freshwater seals (*Pusa sibirica*) that inhabit Russia's Lake Baikal are surmised to have been stranded there when the channel that connected the lake to the Arctic Ocean gradually dried up.

You, gentle reader, are left to judge for yourself which, if any, of these theories is the most plausible.

Kingston, 1881

As early as 1867, but not truly significant until 1881, reports of a strange creature prowling the waters in and around Kingston, where Lake Ontario and the St. Lawrence River meet, began to appear. The 1881 sighting defined the creature that would come to be known as "Kingstie," with witnesses reporting a "sportive creature" about 13 metres long with a head "as big as a small house." One has to wonder who was being sportive—the witnesses or the creature.

In 1934, bathers at nearby Cartwright Bay reported "a strange creature with the head of a dragon and eyes of fire." After procuring a boat and venturing out into the bay to investigate, witnesses reported that the creature had brushed up against their vessel. They couldn't have been looking too closely because in 1979, a group of locals confessed that they had tied a bunch of floating barrels together and affixed a dragon-like head to their very own do-it-yourself cryptid. They anchored it in place and then ran a piece of rope underwater back to the shore where they could tug the twine to make the creature's head bob up and down.

Lake St. Clair, 1897

Separating Ontario and Lake Michigan, Lake St. Clair appears on maps as a lumpy, azure heart tilted slightly to the right. On August 23, 1897, the following account appeared in the *Windsor Evening Record* (reprinted from the *Essex Free Press*):

> *While Miss Ella Burdick and some friends were out fishing on Lake St. Clair, one evening last week at sundown, a dark peculiar-looking object was seen coming up the lake. They rowed very close to the object and were able to get a good look at it. It appeared to have a head somewhat like a dog, with huge eyes protruding and tusk-like projections on each side of the head. Its body appeared to lie some seven or eight feet [2 to 2.5 metres] under water. Some fishermen also saw it and claimed it was some sort of sea serpent. It was certainly a very dangerous and horrible-looking object and was swimming at a very rapid rate.*

Chapter Twenty-two

The Pembroke Wildman

~

On August 1, 1883, the *Newark Daily Advocate* (all the way from Ohio, no less) ran a story nestled half-way down its front page with the headline "Man or Gorilla?" The story reported that the inhabitants of Pembroke had recently been terrified by a "Wildman eight feet [2.4 metres] high and covered with hair." The hirsute savage was ferociously aggressive and inhabited an island in the Ottawa River then known as Prettis, or Prettys, Island for which I can find no present-day reference. Having the appearance of a "man who looks like a gorilla, wandering about in a perfect nude condition and with the exception of the face, completely covered with a thick growth of black hair," this creature or person was definitely not friendly.

Two men called Toughey and Sallman loaded their guns and set off in search of the island-dwelling enigma. At about three o'clock in the afternoon, the creature stomped menacingly out of a thicket brandishing a stone tomahawk in one hand and a heavy cudgel in the other. The Wildman was so terrifying that even though they had guns, the two monster hunters immediately took off back toward their boat. The Wild-man then gave chase, "uttering demonical yells and gesticulat-ing wildly." Hastily scrambling into their boat and casting off, Toughey and Sallman were a short distance from shore when the towering figure lobbed its tomahawk at them with sufficient force and accuracy to fracture Toughey's arm. Sallman fired two shots at the attacker, whereupon he (or it) scrambled off into the woods.

Although it definitely qualifies as a mystery, a subse-quent article in the *Renfrew Mercury* on August 3, 1883, pre-sented evidence that whatever Toughey and Sallman had spotted was human, as if having a tomahawk and a cudgel weren't proof enough. This account told the story of a local family who went to Prettis Island one Saturday to camp over for the night. The father, unable to sleep because of mosquitoes, sat watching the embers of the dying fire. As the fire waned and the shadows encroached, he noticed a massive figure about 2.5 metres tall lurking at the edge of the firelight. The newspaper report said, "His hair was long and shaggy, and hung about his face. He had a vest but no sleeves to his coat, knickerbocker pants, with hairy legs and arms."

The camper spoke to the strange figure, asking it to iden-tify itself. Receiving no answer, he did the only sensible thing and threw a rock at the interloper, causing it to retreat.

It is not clear which of these two encounters took place first. One can't help but wonder if the camper's lobbing of

MAN OR GORILLA?

The Extraordinary Character Who is Scaring Canucks.

OTTAWA, ONT., Aug. 1. — Pembroke, about one hundred miles north of Ottawa has a lively sensation in the shape of a wild man eight feet high and covered with hair. His haunts are on Prettis Island, a short distance from the town, and the people are so terrified that no one has dared to venture on the island for several weeks. Two raftsmen named Toughey and Sallman, armed with weapons, plucked up sufficient courage to scour the woods in hope of seeing the monster. About 3 o'clock in the afternoon their curiosity was rewarded. He emerged from a thicket having in one hand a tomahawk made of stone and in the other a bludgeon. His appearance struck such terror to the hearts of the raftsmen that they made tracks for the boat which was moored by the beach. The giant followed them, uttering demoniacal yells and gesticulating wildly. They had barely time to get into the boat and pull a short distance out into the stream when he hurled the tomahawk after them, striking Toughey in the arm and fracturing it. Sallman fired two shots, but neither took effect, the giant retreating hurriedly at the first sound of firearms. It is more than probable that the townspeople will arrange an expedition to capture, if possible, what Toughey describes as a man who looks like a gorilla, wandering about in a perfectly nude condition, and, with the exception of the face, completely covered with a thick growth of black hair.

"Man or Gorilla?" The article as it originally appeared in the *Newark Daily Advocate* on August 1, 1883 a stone at the unfriendly giant was what prompted the attack on Toughey and Sallman. Either way, the presence of clothes and tools pretty much mark this as an encounter between humans and not a meeting with a creature heretofore unknown to science. But, assuming that the events occurred as reported and were neither part of a hoax nor some sort of mass confabulation, who was this feral giant? How and why did he come to be on the island? Why are there no further accounts of him? Was he a transient? What can account for his seemingly variable temperament?

Who was he?

Chapter Twenty-three

Old Yellow Top Sightings, a.k.a. Precambrian Shield Man

~

Of all the mysteries in this book, this writer is most drawn to those that involve creatures unknown to science—"monsters" in the vernacular and "cryptids" according to the designation grudgingly bestowed upon them by the scientific establishment. But the establishment is quick to point out that just because we've given them a cool name, that doesn't mean they exist. And therein lies the source of the sense of wonder and hope that many people find in the idea of unknown creatures—the possibility that in spite of our many scientific, technological and medical marvels, in spite of our smug, self-assumed mastery of our planet, there could still be mysterious and as-yet-undiscovered creatures lurking not in the distant ocean depths, but treading through the same woods, fields and shadows as ourselves.

The study of creatures unrecognized by mainstream science is called "cryptozoology," but it's not something you can go out and get a degree in. Furthermore, the presumed existence of certain cryptids presupposes not merely a new genus or species of animals already known to exist (for example, a new genus of giant squid or a new species of aye-aye), but rather, an entirely new *family* of creatures—and that is why mainstream science quite rightly has trouble with the idea. Cryptids are, by their very nature, unclassifiable, having their roots in mythology, legend and folklore. In short, their existence is supposed but unproven, and that is why they are fascinating.

Stories of hairy, ape-like creatures are a long, looming presence in the oral traditions of our First Nations. Many different spirits, entities and names have been associated with the cryptid known today as Bigfoot or Sasquatch. For example, Tsonoqua is a mercurial, child-stealing ogress in the West Coast tradition. Bukwas is a wildman of the woods. The Seeahtiks were a supposed tribe of ferocious giants said to inhabit Washington State. Legends and sightings of Sasquatch are predominantly West Coast phenomena, but there have been Bigfoot sightings all across Canada.

Ontario, of course, has enjoyed its share of "bipedal hairy hominid" sightings, just not as prolifically as British Columbia. The community of Cobalt, in the Timiskaming District, made its mark in Ontario as a mining town. Silver was discovered in the area in 1903, and three years after that, the creature known alternately as "Precambrian Shield Man" and "Yellow Top" was first sighted.

In 1906, several men building the head frame (the structure at the mouth of a mine) at the Violet Mine, just east of

Cobalt, reported seeing an ape-like creature with a mane of light-coloured hair or fur around its head, leading to the nickname "Yellow Top." There were no further sightings until late July 1927. On this occasion, miners J.A. MacAuley and Lorne Wilson reported seeing a similar animal. While pulling ore samples from their claims northeast of the Wettlaufer Mine, they saw what seemed to be a bear browsing for food in a nearby blueberry patch. Wilson threw a stone at it whereupon, according to him, "It kind of stood up and growled at us. Then it ran away. It sure was like no bear that I have ever seen. Its head was kind of yellow and the rest of it was black like a bear, all covered with hair."

In this case, one can't help but wonder if it actually was a bear. In 2009, a zoo in Germany was baffled by the sorry state of Dolores, one of its spectacled bears. She lost most of her fur except for a ruff around her face, turning from a rather cute-looking creature into one of horrifying aspect, more a monster than a bear. Although spectacled bears are not native to North America, it could be possible that a member of the local bruin population had fallen prey to similar disorder.

After the July 1927 sighting, Yellow Top appears to have gone to ground for 19 years, not appearing again until April 1946. A woman and her son were walking from their home near Gillies Depot along the railway tracks into Cobalt. Suddenly, the woman spotted a strange figure moving unhurriedly off the tracks and into the surrounding trees. It was covered in dark fur or hair, but it had a light-coloured head and walked in a nearly human fashion. Skeptical readers would be correct to point out that bears are quite capable of bipedal locomotion for several steps and not in a tottering fashion, either—they can walk on two legs with great assurance, but do so only rarely. The "light" head is, as always, puzzling.

Another 29 years went by before Yellow Top put in its next appearance, but this time, it was far more dramatic. One night, in early August 1975, 27 miners were on their way by bus to the overnight shift at the Cobalt Lode mine. Suddenly, the bus driver, Amee Latreille, seemed to lose control of the bus, and it came close to careening down a nearby rock cut. When the shaken miners asked what had happened, Mr. Latreille said he had been startled by a dark figure crossing the road directly in front of the bus.

"At first I thought it was a big bear," he said. "But then it turned to face the headlights and I could see some light hair, almost down to the shoulders. It couldn't have been a bear." Latreille was so shaken, he said he did not know if he would continue to drive the route.

A miner at the front of the bus, Larry Cormack, an averred non-believer in Precambrian Shield Man, said that it "looked like a bear to me at first, but it didn't walk like one. It was kind of half stooped over. Maybe it was a wounded bear, I don't know."

Whatever Yellow Top is, the scarcity of its appearances makes it more elusive even than Sasquatch. Not to be a complete party-pooper here, but the fact that everyone says it looks like a bear would seem to suggest that the creature is, in fact, a bear, or rather, a succession of bears over the years, each perhaps suffering from some disfiguring ursine disease or injury. Still, one can't help but be envious of people who are privileged to see something that takes them, even if only for few seconds, completely outside their usual worldview and into the freedom and wonder of the unknown.

Chapter Twenty-four

Mid-20th-Century Lake Monsters and the Birth of Igopogo

Miminiska Lake, 1947

Located more or less in the very centre of Ontario, the little community of Miminiska lies at a widening of the Albany River. For eager anglers, it has been an important fishing destination since the early part of the 20th century. In the 1940s, the local population was a mixture of Cree and white inhabitants, all living off the land and making extra money guiding greenhorn fishermen through the waters of Miminiska Lake. The following story was related by ex-Lieutenant Mike ("Smoky") Lewicky, an expert marksman who served overseas for two years during World War II and who then built a lodge at the point of the lake on his return to Canada. He told the story to *Globe and Mail* reporter Jack Hambleton, who travelled to the area in August 1947.

Just a couple of hundred metres from Lewicky's new fishing lodge was a Cree band, many members of which were hired by Lewicky to help construct his lodge. While the menfolk were thus occupied during the day, the women of the band tended to the "night lines," nets set to capture the many sturgeon that populated the depths of Miminiska Lake. Once caught, the big fish were flown to the nearby community of Natina, where they were processed and then shipped to the United States. Sturgeon sales were an important source of income for the band. One of the women who did this work, Mrs. Sagetchaway, was widely respected in the area.

One evening, Lewicky was surprised when Mrs. Sagetchaway burst into his lodge, trembling with agitation and so scared that she seemed "almost out of her mind" with fear. She told Lewicky that she had seen a creature "resembling a big snake. It was as big as a barrel and seemed to her about 50 feet [15 metres] long. The head was covered with hair, and the thing had a mane like a horse. It undulated as it went through the water but made no effort to attack her." The men in the community shrugged off the story, but not for long.

A short time later, a Cree fisherman named Daniel Wapoos was out alone in a motorized canoe when he, too, spotted the "thing," later saying it was too horrible to describe. In any event, upon seeing it, he wasn't inclined to stick around looking for details, but high-tailed it back to land as fast as he could. Lewicky armed himself with a rifle and revolver and set out on the lake to look for the creature. He found nothing and was starting to wonder if Sagetchaway and Wapoos were having a bit of fun with him. But the next day, Daniel Wapoos' brother, Andrew, burst into the lodge with a similar story. He had seen something as big around as a barrel frolicking in one of the lake's shallow bays.

Possibly lured by the presence of Jack Hambleton, the *Globe and Mail* reporter, a sort of deputation now descended upon the little community. The group included Deputy Minister Frank MacDougall, who came all the way from Toronto; Keith Atcheson, the district forester at Sioux Lookout; and Eugene Girton, the chief ranger at Pickle Lake. The three officials took Hambleton up in a small plane to survey the district from the air, and then all four men set out in two boats to observe the sturgeon fishing. The following passage is Hambleton's somewhat underwhelming but cogently written eyewitness account:

> *En route back to camp about 5 PM, all four saw a terrific splashing in a shallow bay about a mile north. There was a heavy wind blowing away from the bay, and the splashing was loud enough to be heard even at a mile. Nothing could be seen however, but the water going high into the air. It was not a moose, for a moose could have been seen. Sturgeon characteristics include a rolling or porpoising in shallow water with some splashing, but if a sturgeon caused this splashing, it must have been of a terrific size, and a 70-pound [32-kilogram] sturgeon is a big fish on the*

*Albany, although in coastal Great Lakes water they some-
times attain a weight of several hundred pounds.*

Whatever the creature was, the sense of fear in the community was real and palpable. The Cree spoke of a mythical lake
denizn called Nani-bajou and took extra care when travelling on
the lake, also keeping their children close to camp. Even though
he had never seen it himself, Mike Lewicky urged his wife and
six-year-old son to exercise caution. In the end, Deputy Minister
MacDougall went back to Toronto. Officials Girton and
Atcheson were advised by their superiors to keep an eye out for
the monster and, if possible, take photographs—they accepted
their assignment without any great show of enthusiasm. And,
for his part, Jack Hambleton wrote in conclusion that he didn't
"want any part of it, not having lost any mysterious monsters
on Miminiska."

Sutton, 1952: The Birth of Igopogo, a.k.a. Kempenfelt Kelly

On August 1, 1952, fishing guide Wellington Charles
was doing what he had been doing for 50 years—taking sightseers on a boat tour through the waters of Lake Simcoe. His
passengers were Mrs. Pauline Nichol and her 10-year-old daughter, June, from Toronto. Along for the ride was another young
girl, unnamed in the newspaper accounts. Off the shores of
Georgina Island, the three passengers suddenly exclaimed
together because they had all seen a large animal swimming

through the water. Wellington Charles didn't see it but told them it was probably an otter. However, a few minutes later, Charles himself saw the thing and had to admit that it looked like nothing he had ever seen in all his years on the water. Newspaper accounts described the creature as "having a head about the size and shape of a bulldog's, with shiny, black fur."

Charles, who had trapped many an otter in his time, was adamant that it was not an otter, nor had he ever trapped anything that even remotely resembled the creature. An article that appeared in the *Globe and Mail* on August 2, 1952, concluded with a tip of the hat to Charles, stating, "he has named it the Igopogo, which is not to be confused with the Ogopogo of western legend."

And that, in a nutshell, is the first recorded sighting of Igopogo by that name. Some reports spuriously assert that the moniker Igopogo was given to the supposed beast by First Nations observers, long before the arrival of Europeans, but this is pure bunk. As the article mentioned above clearly shows, Igopogo was named *after* white men first gave the name Ogopogo to the creature known to the First Nations as Naitaka. The name Ogopogo is generally accepted as having been taken from a 1924 music hall song, "The Ogopogo: The Funny Foxtrot," with words by Cumberland Clark and music by Mark Strong. It describes the search for a strange creature whose mother was an earwig and whose father was a whale.

As to why Wellington Charles should have specifically chosen "Igopogo" as his monster's name, my own personal theory is as follows. In 1952, when Charles and the Nichols saw the creature swimming in Lake Simcoe, the U.S. was gearing up for a presidential election in which Republican Dwight D. Eisenhower was squaring off against Democrat Adlai Stevenson. The Eisenhower campaign harnessed the power of a simple slogan that appeared on thousands of buttons: "I like Ike." Not to be outdone, fans of the comic strip *Pogo*, an often-political satire that recounted the adventures of its titular swamp-dwelling possum, responded by creating their own slogan: "I Go Pogo." Indeed, in 1952, a paperback anthology of the comic strip was published under this very name. *Pogo* was also very popular in Canada—the copy of *I Go Pogo* that I possess has a cheerful yellow cover and a crumbling price tag on the back that reads, "In Canada—$1.50." When the time came to name the creature he had seen, Charles chose a name that echoed Ogopogo, but had a much more current and humorous connotation.

That, then, is my personal theory as to where the name Igopogo comes from. True or not, it is certainly more plausible than the notion that a First Nations group bestowed the name on the supposed beastie.

The creature's subsequent rechristening to "Kempenfelt Kelly" is decidedly unfortunate. The name Igopogo is bouncy and eccentric, whereas Kelly is someone you hire from a temp agency. One suspects that the name Kelly was simply more readily identifiable on souvenir T-shirts in and around Kempenfelt Bay near Barrie, where the creature has also been spotted. At any rate, the renaming has done nothing to materialize concrete proof of the lake monster's existence. In the public imagination, Igopogo has grown from a furry mammal with the face of a bulldog to an all-out "sea" monster with a serpent-like body, an undulating neck and gigantic fins. There have, of course, been myriad sightings through the years, but so far nothing that one could rightly call proof.

Chapter Twenty-five

The Beast of the Side Roads

~

On August 14, 1965, a trucker was driving down the highway just past Smithsville, near Hamilton, when he had to turn onto a side road to avoid an overpass that was too low for his truck. Once on the smaller road, he was shocked to see, standing in the middle of the road, what he later described as a "half-human, half-animal beast—six or seven feet [about two metres] tall." He estimated that it must have weighed 500 pounds [227 kilograms]. The *Hamilton Spectator* reported that it had "broad shoulders, a small head and long arms." The driver looked down to change gears, and when he raised his head again, the apparition was gone.

In those days, long before the advent of "Don't Drink and Drive," the *Spectator* pointedly headlined the story "Teetotal Trucker Spots 'Monster.'" It also quoted his wife as saying, "My husband doesn't drink and he wasn't tired that night—he said if he had had a weak heart he would have died on the spot. He won't go back at night but he is going back to check for tracks in the daytime."

Three days later, on August 17, another short article appeared describing the chaos that the sighting had created for the local detachment of the Ontario Provincial Police (OPP). Although there were no additional sightings, the OPP were swamped with calls about the supposed beast. Furthermore, although the OPP had been unable to discover a single concrete trace of the creature, one frustrated officer noted that rumours were spreading that the police *had* found evidence, "We've even heard reports that we've measured the tracks and they are 16 inches [40.5 centimetres] long." About a week later, there were more sightings about 11 kilometres away in Campden, but they were all similarly inconclusive. There were also additional, unverified reports of tracks measuring 16 inches in length. And that was it—the monster slipped quietly into the pages of history and continued anonymity.

A bit of perspective is important. Although this case pops up on all sorts of Bigfoot websites and books, each article is tiny—150 words long, if that. There was bigger news in 1965, after all—Los Angeles was in the grip of violent and destructive riots born of racial tension, and The Beatles had just played their tumultuous concert at Shea Stadium and were heading to Toronto for shows at Maple Leaf Gardens. A strange creature in Ontario was not a major story.

I feel that it's important to point out that *none* of the books or websites citing the original articles gives the correct dates of publication. In fact, several different dates are given, all of them wrong. Finally, after scouring issues of the *Hamilton Spectator* for the entire month of August 1965, I found the articles, which were dated August 14 and 17. While this is, of course, only one case, it doesn't exactly inspire confidence that due diligence is being exercised. My point is that if you're thinking of taking an interest in cryptozoology, please check *all* of your sources and list them clearly. Remember, everyone *already* thinks you're crazy—don't give them any ammunition to suggest that you're also incompetent.

An interesting sidelight here is the difference between this and a similar series of concurrent sightings that happened south of the border in Monroe, Michigan. From June to August 1975, the Monroe Monster was spotted by about 15 people and was described as being approximately seven feet (2.1 metres) tall, covered in black hair and weighing about 400 pounds (181 kilograms). In the middle of August, just as the sightings near Hamilton were taking place, about 1000 Monroe locals banded together to hunt down the Michigan creature. The entire mob waded menacingly through the swampy area that the beast was supposed to inhabit. Needless to say, they were not successful. Meanwhile, back in Canada, we took a polite, if brief interest in our monster and then let it go on its merry way. Yay, Canada!

Chapter Twenty-six

Monster Busters!

~

Muskrat Lake lies close to the Ontario-Québec border, about 100 kilometres northwest of Ottawa. It is 16 kilometres long, 1.6 kilometres wide and its depth ranges from 18 to 60 metres. In other words, as far as Ontario lakes go, it is neither particularly large, nor is it particularly deep—in fact, one could say it is both small and shallow. Nevertheless, this little strip of fresh water is the purported home of "Mussie," an aquatic cryptid of surprisingly variable shape and size.

In the autumn of 1988, author Michael Bradley and two companions set out in a small, custom-built boat to search for the beast. Over the course of a few weeks, they sailed the misty waters of Muskrat Lake, looking for answers but finding only more questions. Bradley's direct contact with the supposed creature was limited at best—an anomalous sonar reading on October 5, 1988, which he interpreted to be two large creatures swimming toward the surface, and one distant sighting through binoculars that Bradley himself said was inconclusive. Consequently, the book that Bradley wrote about his experiences,

More Than a Myth: The Search for the Monster of Muskrat Lake, has little to do with Mussie and everything to do with lake monsters in general. Nevertheless, it is a thoughtful, if at times farfetched meditation on underwater cryptids and hypothetical "maybes" regarding the Muskrat Lake mystery.

Although local lore says that First Nations observers related accounts of the lake beast to Samuel de Champlain in the early 17th century, there are no accounts in de Champlain's journals to support this. Bradley interviewed several eyewitnesses and their accounts of the creature more or less tallied. In sightings ranging from 1968 to 1988, the creature was generally described as being about 2 to 3.5 metres long, with a rounded head and a much larger, rounded body. In *no* accounts does it have a long, lizard-like neck. Its colouring ranges from "silver green" to "dusky red." In a 1976 sighting, the creature was described as having smooth skin, whereas in a separate, later sighting, it appeared to possibly have fine fur that was shiny and slick. The creature's rather unremarkable physiognomy included a rounded forehead and a short snout with, according to one witness, "endearing" brown eyes. It was often observed swimming along, its head or back protruding 25 to 30 centimetres out of the water, but in one instance, it was observed to create a whirlpool about four metres in diameter. One witness who had observed Mussie at a fair distance, out of the water on a beach, said it also appeared to have fins, on the front, at least. Someone else said it also had a long tooth drooping lopsidedly out of one side of its mouth. If anything, the descriptions seemed to suggest a large and somewhat overweight seal; indeed, Bradley at one point mused that Mussie could be a relict species of freshwater walrus or seal.

What could it be that fishermen and boaters on Muskrat Lake have been seeing? To his credit, Bradley spells out a number of options along with pros and cons for each. The first theory, that old humbug of monster-spotters down through the ages, is that the sightings are merely waves. In small bays or narrow bodies of water such as Muskrat Lake, rolling waves can play strange tricks upon the eye, often seeming to be the hump of a submerged serpent or appearing to be a solid, moving mass, such as the back of a large, swimming, underwater beast. For his own satisfaction, Bradley succeeded in creating such waves on Lake Muskrat; the rolling water of his boat's wake bounced off both shores, rolled back to the middle of the lake and met there with every appearance of being a serpent-bodied creature frolicking in the water. In the right circumstances, such waves may appear several minutes *after* the vessel that created them has left the area. Indeed, most of the lake monster videos currently making their way around the Internet are rather obviously waves.

Bradley's book is valuable for its careful consideration of what *kind* of creature could possibly live undetected for centuries beneath the surface of a small lake. Some type of amphibious species would make the most sense, since the ability of such a creature to breathe underwater would mean that it would not need to surface for air, thus minimizing opportunities for humans to see or capture it. While a giant species of Chinese salamander (*Andrias davidiaunus*) can, *in extremely rare cases*, reach two metres in length, the largest species native to North America is the hellbender salamander (*Cryptobranchus allegan-iensis*), which can only reach a length of 60 centimetres, far smaller than any of the observed sightings of Mussie.

Rejected out of hand is the notion that the creature could be some sort of large, exothermic (cold-blooded) species because the cool temperatures of the lake would make the creature so slow and sluggish that it could not move fast enough to hunt or elude capture. Readers are advised to bear in mind that fish are cold-blooded and do just fine in cold lake waters. For instance, sturgeon (a type of large, cold-blooded fish) are often suggested as a possible candidate for Mussie sightings, but Bradley dismisses this possibility. He points out that, as of 1988, no sturgeon have been found there for 20 years, citing a 1968 study by Ontario's Ministry of Natural Resources that concludes there are no sturgeon present in the lake. However, according to a 2002 study by the Fisheries Section of the Ontario government, Muskrat Lake *does* have sturgeon. Although North American sturgeon do not typically reach the size of the European record holder—nearly six metres—extraordinary specimens can grow to lengths of two to three metres. Moreover, sturgeon are some of the longest-lived fish in the world, often reaching 100 years or more in age. While it is *highly unlikely* that one or more sturgeon of this size could live undetected in Muskrat

Lake, it is mentioned here to point out a curious circularity in the thought processes of many monster hunters—the notion that an *unknown* animal could escape detection for *thousands of years* is posited to be *more likely* than the possibility of a *known* species escaping detection for a *couple of decades*.

Bradley suggests that Mussie could be a relict species of plesiosaur, a warm-blooded dinosaur with a small head, long, thin neck, thick body and flippers—the type of creature most often assumed to be the Loch Ness Monster. But to get around the obvious difficulties, namely that such a creature would need to surface in order to breathe and so be subject to observation by humans, Bradley cites fossil remains of a plesiosaur-like creature with a snorkel-like breathing tube that would have allowed it to remain submerged even as it breathed air.

We shall pass over Mr. Bradley's decidedly unorthodox views on the historical existence of dragons. We shall also refrain from commenting on his avowed belief in the existence of an Australian worm four metres long and as thick as a man's thigh. However, his book presents instructive points of view as they pertain to his final theory on what may lie below the surface of Muskrat Lake. Bradley posits that UFOs, the existence of which he takes as a near-given, are the emissaries of water-dwelling alien intelligences so powerful that they can "project" manifestations of their own consciousness in the form of "greys," the light-skinned, large-eyed aliens of recent popularity. How exactly these alien intelligences relate to the world's myriad lake monsters remains unclear, but Bradley tenuously connects them to Stonehenge, cattle mutilations, crop circles and "dragon flight paths." The upshot seems to be that the Loch Ness Monster, and by extension, Mussie, are from outer space.

It feels disingenuous to criticize the conclusions, however doubtful, of someone who has actually been to Muskrat Lake and collected first-hand evidence and testimony. However, it would be equally disingenuous to suggest that I in any way concur with them. Until the capture of an actual specimen, dead or alive, the identity of Mussie will remain a mystery.

Sturgeon, anyone?

Chapter Twenty-seven

Giant Footprints in the Far North

~

Polar Bear Provincial Park lies in Ontario's far north, on the western shore of Hudson Bay where it dips south to become James Bay. It is the province's largest park, with an area of more than 22,000 square kilometres. There are no tourist facilities, and anyone wishing to fly into the park must first get permission from one of the park's four airstrips. Straddling the treeline, Polar Bear Provincial Park is a vast, desolate area of rolling tundra and swampy muskeg. Its inhabitants are, not surprisingly, polar bears, as well as some seals and walruses along the coast.

There is also a small community called Peawanuck. About 250 people live in Peawanuck, all members of the Weenusk First Nation (sometimes spelled "Winisk"). A thousand years ago, the Algonquin lived in the region, and now, their Cree descendants are the citizens of Peawanuck. It is a remote community of people accustomed to their rugged environment and well acquainted with the limited wildlife it supports.

On June 9, 2001, a member of the Weenusk band was travelling through the bush on a four-wheel, all-terrain vehicle and spotted an odd trail of huge tracks, each one 35 centimetres long and 12 centimetres wide. Chief Abraham Hunter was adamant that the tracks could not have been from a bear. "I looked at them. They were six feet [two metres] apart, walking." In the midst of the barren landscape, the novelty of the cryptic tracks gripped the tightknit community for a few days, but the fascination soon wore off, and life went back to normal.

On June 14, the Ministry of Natural Resources sent investigators to photograph the tracks. They also found another odd-looking print 100 kilometres east of Peawanuck. Ministry spokesman Brent Kelly admitted that it was tempting to jump to conclusions, but it was equally important to stick to the facts. "There's no idea what it is," he said. "We don't want to jump and down and say 'Bigfoot! Bigfoot!' but there's some strange tracks up there and we are curious."

Weenusk official John Wabano brushed aside the idea that the tracks could have been made by a bear, saying, "I don't think any animal could make a print like that."

Brent Kelly pointed out that if the tracks were a hoax, it would have been a very expensive one because of the huge distances involved. Wabano concurred, saying, "I don't think anyone would be able to make tracks all over the place in such a vast area." He added, "It is real. It's been sighted before [referring to a sighting in 1976]. I guess he's always been out there. We assume that it's just passing through like last time."

And that is where the case rests. Will the mysterious tracks reappear in 2021? Sooner? Never? Is there really a solitary wanderer, alone in the wilderness, nomadically treading the tundra? Whatever the truth of the matter is, believers are left with an image that is somewhat sad and rather romantic—a mysterious, solitary figure roaming the lonely north, one two-metre-long stride at a time.

Chapter Twenty-eight

The Giant of Grassy Narrows

~

I n the Algonquian tradition, the Wendigo is an evil, canni-
balistic spirit. The many tribes and nations of the Algonquin each have their own variation of how a Wendigo
behaves or manifests itself. In many of the variants, humans can
become Wendigos if they eat the flesh of other humans, and
such individuals become feared outcasts. The Montagnais of
Labrador believed the Wendigos to be flesh-eating giants 4.5 to
6 metres tall. By the middle of the 20th century, the Wendigo
had become one of the First Nations entities that was, rightly or
wrongly, often associated with Bigfoot. In 1963, an article in *BC
Digest* reflected that "Some of the old accounts of Wendigos in
the northwest describe apparitions more in accord in description
and behaviour with the Sasquatch...than with the traditional
wendigo or *weetigo* of the Cree Algonkian tribesman."

It is interesting, then, when humanoid creatures are
sighted on or near First Nations reserves, there is a general tendency to avoid labels such as "Bigfoot" or "Sasquatch." Usually,
witnesses, though amazed, simply say they have not seen anything like it before. Often, a previous sighting that occurred

THE GIANT OF GRASSY NARROWS

269

years or even decades earlier is recalled, and the connection to some kind of tradition often seems as important as the sighting itself. The Grassy Narrows incident is a case such as this.

◇

On Tuesday, July 22, 2008, Helen Pahpasay and her mother, Agnes, were driving north from their home on the Grassy Narrows First Nation Reserve near Kenora. It was about 10 o'clock in the morning, and they were heading off to go blueberry picking. Suddenly, about 15 metres ahead of the their truck, they saw a dark, hulking figure strolling toward them. Helen said, "It was black, about eight feet [2.4 metres] long and all black, and the way it walked was upright, human-like, but more—I don't know how to describe it—more of a husky walk, I guess….It didn't look normal."

Thinking she must be seeing things, Helen looked over at Agnes only to see that her mother was rubbing her eyes before peering once more at the baffling sight in front of them. Tall and lanky, the creature continued to amble toward their truck. "It was walking casually. I know it wasn't an animal 'cause it was upright," Helen said, adding, "It wasn't a bear or a moose."

The creature seemed to spot them and went crashing into the nearby woods, where they lost sight of it. "We were scared," said Helen. They were so scared that she and Agnes turned the truck around and drove back to Grassy Narrows, hearts pounding all the way. Back home, the shaken witnesses told Helen's brother, Randy Fobister, and his family what they had seen.

Far from being spooked, Randy wanted to go back and look for the creature, later telling reporters, "We were just excited. I kept hearing about this thing. I've been hearing about it since I was a kid, so when I got the chance close by here, I jumped right on it."

So they all piled back into the truck and found the spot where Helen and Agnes had sighted the strange figure. There, close to a beaver dam and pond, they found a single, large, six-toed footprint. To judge from the footprint's location next to the beaver dam, the creature appeared to have taken one huge step over the dam and into the pond, where, of course, it would have been fruitless to search for more tracks.

They took a cast of the footprint, which gave a much clearer picture of whatever it was that had made the impression. Measuring 38 centimetres long by 15 centimetres wide, the plaster cast shows a huge heel with an equally massive big toe, about as wide as three fingers. The family stored the cast away in a pizza box, since that was the only container they could find that would fit it.

Grassy Narrows has a tradition of creature sightings. Randy Fobister had been hearing about them since he was a child. Every few years, there would be a report of a sighting, sometimes accompanied by terrifying bestial screams. For her part, Helen Pahpasay says, "There's been talk of Bigfoot, Sasquatch. And I'm still not sure what it was, but I've never seen anything like it before."

~

The argument goes like this—if Bigfoot exists, by now someone should have found concrete proof such as bones, hides, a corpse, *something*. To counter this, believers cite species such as the coelacanth, a deep-ocean fish thought to have been extinct for more than 70 million years until someone hauled one up in a net in 1938. Or they refer to those increasingly rare pockets of humanity that have had no interaction with modern society (often choosing to ignore the fact that "modern society" knows where these people are and is doing everything it can to leave them alone). Still, say the skeptics, isn't it odd that after hundreds of years of sightings, a population of creatures large enough to survive has managed to do such a remarkable job of hiding all traces of their existence—feces, the bodies of deceased individuals and so forth? And, really, wouldn't we expect a creature of this sort to appear in the fossil record? Until there is rock-hard proof, either the capture of a living individual or the discovery of a body, Bigfoot's value to science is nil.

Culturally, Bigfoot represents the uncertainty that lies at the heart of the debate between skeptics and believers. As long as this creature, if it exists, remains a mystery, believers have something to hope for, a quest to undertake, a Holy Grail for which to search. And skeptics can continue to disbelieve. The beauty of this model is that even if a hairy, stomping, snorting

specimen is captured tomorrow, it would still become a light-
ning rod for amazement and wonder. After all, if creatures so
remarkable, so massive and so similar to ourselves can lead
a furtive existence for thousands of years, defying science, prob-
ability and logic in the process, then surely we live in a world of
unlimited possibility, rich with mystery and buoyed by hope.

Notes on Sources

Chapter 1: The Peterborough Petroglyphs

"Archaeoacoustics: Spirits in the Stones." *Fortean Times*, October 2004. www.
forteantimes.com/fetures/articles/143/archaeoacoustics_spirits_in_the_
stones.html (retrieved 20 January 2012).

Vastokas, Joan M., and K. Romas. *Sacred Art of the Algonkians: A Study of the
Peterborough Petroglyphs*. Peterborough: Mansard Press, 1973.

Chapter 2: The Serpent Mound

Johnston, Richard B. *The Archaeology of the Serpent Mounds Site*. Toronto: Royal
Ontario Museum (University of Toronto), 1968.

Kenyon, W.A. *Mounds of Sacred Earth: Burial Mounds of Ontario*. Publications in
Archaeology (Monograph 9). Toronto: Royal Ontario Museum, 1986.

Chapter 3: The Baldoon Mystery

Colombo, John Robert. *Mysteries of Ontario*. Toronto: Hounslow Press, 1999.

McDonald, Neil T. *The Baldoon Mystery*. Alan Mann, ed. (Neil T. McDonald's
account was originally published as *The Belledoon Mysteries*). Wallaceburg:
Standard Press, 1986.

www.ontarioplaques.com/Plaques_ABC/Plaque_ChathamKent18.html.

Chapter 4: The Spectral Lights of Cornwall

"The Marsh Point Ghosts." *New Dominion Monthly*, November 1869. www.
ghosttownpix.com/lostvillages/millroch.html (Retrieved 20 January 2012).

Chapter 5: The Ghost of University College

Bissell, Claude T. (ed.) *University College: A Portrait, 1853–1953*. Toronto: University of Toronto Press, 1953.

Loudon, W.J. *Studies of Student Life, Volume V: The Golden Age*. Toronto: University of Toronto Press, 1928.

Richardson, Douglas. *A Not Unsightly Building: University College and Its History*.
Toronto: Mosaic Press for University College, 1990.

Chapter 6: William Lyon Mackenzie King: The Prime Minister Who Spoke with the Dead

Esberey, Joy E. *Knight of the Holy Spirit: A Study of William Lyon Mackenzie King.* Toronto: University of Toronto Press, 1980.

Levine, Allan. *King: William Lyon Mackenzie King: A Life Guided by the Hand of Destiny.* Vancouver/Toronto: Douglas & McIntyre, 2011.

Stacey, C.P. A *Very Double Life: The Private World of Mackenzie King.* Toronto: Macmillan Company of Canada, 1976.

Library and Archives Canada. "A Real Companion and Friend: The Diary of William Lyon Mackenzie King." www.collectionscanada.gc.ca/king/index-e.html.

Library and Archives Canada. "The Diaries of William Lyon Mackenzie King" (searchable database). www.collectionscanada.gc.ca/databases/king/001059-100.01-e.php.

Library and Archives Canada. "Companions from Another World" (notes from Mackenzie King's séance on 6 October 1935). www.collectionscanada.gc.ca/2/4/h4-2316.1-e.html.

Chapter 7: The Girl Who Had Lived Before

Stearn, Jess. *The Search for the Girl with the Blue Eyes.* Garden City, NY: Doubleday, 1968.

Chapter 8: A Haunting in the Suburbs

"Eight Flee Home's Screeching Ghost." *Toronto Telegram*, 8 May 1968.

"Teens Taunt at Haunted House as Spirit Spreads New Terror." *Toronto Telegram*, 9 May 1968.

"Hawkins Family to Quit that Haunted Etobicoke House." *Toronto Telegram*, 22 May 1968.

Chapter 9: The God Helmet

Biography of Dr. Michael Persinger, Psychology Depatment, Laurentian University. www.laurentian.ca/Laurentian/Home/Departments/Psychology/Faculty+List/Michael+Persinger/Dr.+Michael+Persinger.htm?Laurentian_Lang=en-CA (retrieved 30 January 2012).

"Close encounters of the neurological kind." *Globe and Mail*, 26 November 1995.

"This Is Your Brain on God." *Wired*, Issue 7.11, November 1999. www.wired.com/wired/archive/7.11/persinger.html (retrieved 20 January 2012).

Chapter 10: The Airborne Menace

Rutkowski, Chris, and Geoff Dittman. *The Canadian UFO Report: The Best Cases Revealed.* Toronto: Dundurn Press, 2006.

Chapter 11. Project Magnet

MUFON Ontario Archives. www.virtuallystrange.net/ufo/mufonontario/archive/wbsmith.htm.

Rutkowski, Chris, and Geoff Dittman. *The Canadian UFO Report: The Best Cases Revealed.* Toronto: Dundurn Press, 2006.

Chapter 12: Close Encounters in Ontario

"The Extraterrestrial Therapist." *Saturday Night*, 3 June 1995.

Rutkowski, Chris, and Geoff Dittman. *The Canadian UFO Report: The Best Cases Revealed.* Toronto: Dundurn Press, 2006.

Chapter 13. The Carp UFO

MUFON Ontario Archives. www.virtuallystrange.net/ufo/mufonontario/archive/carp.htm.

Rutkowski, Chris, and Geoff Dittman. *The Canadian UFO Report: The Best Cases Revealed.* Toronto: Dundurn Press, 2006.

Chapter 14: Still Closer Encounters

"Dark Side of the Unknown." *Omni*, 1 September 1993.

"The Extraterrestrial Therapist." *Saturday Night*, 3 June 1995.

Rutkowski, Chris. *Abductions & Aliens: What's Really Going On?* Toronto: Dundurn Press, 1999.

Rutkowski, Chris, and Geoff Dittman. *The Canadian UFO Report: The Best Cases Revealed.* Toronto: Dundurn Press, 2006.

Chapter 15: The Kinrade Murder

"Who Shot Ethel Kinrade?" *Hamilton Spectator*, 26 February 1909.

"How 'Down and Outs' Impose on the Public." *Hamilton Spectator*, 27 February 1909.

"Ways of Getting Rid of the Tramp Nuisance." *Hamilton Spectator*, 1 March 1909.

"Well Known in Virginia." *Hamilton Spectator*, 3 March 1909.

"Important Developments in Kinrade Murder Case." *Hamilton Spectator*, 8 March 1909.

"Love Letters Were Not For The Public." *Hamilton Spectator*, 4 May 1909.

"Pertinent and Impertinent." *Hamilton Spectator*, 5 May 1909.

"Bedfort is Discharged." *New York Times*, 16 November 1909.

Charlesworth, Hector. *More Candid Chronicles: Further leaves from the Note Book of a Canadian Journalist.* Toronto: Macmillan Company of Canada, 1928.

Wallace, W. Stewart. *Murders and mysteries, a Canadian series.* Westport, CT: Hyperion Press, 1975.

Chapter 16: The Death of Tom Thomson

MacGregor, Roy. *Northern Light: The Enduring Mystery of Tom Thomson and the Woman Who Loved Him.* Toronto: Random House Canada, 2010.

Town, Harold, and David P. Silcox. *Tom Thomson: The Silence and the Storm.* Toronto: McClelland and Stewart, 1977.

Chapter 17: The Disappearance of Ambrose Small

McClement, Fred. *The Strange Case of Ambrose Small.* Toronto: McClelland and Stewart, 1974.

RG 4-123, Files of the Department of the Attorney General relating to Ambrose Small. Archives of Ontario.

Chapter 18: The Disappearance of Rocco Perri

"Starkman, Besha (Bessie)." Dictionary of Canadian Biography Online. www.biographi.ca/009004-119.01-e.php?&id_nbr=8372&&PHPSESSID=ychzfqkvzape (retrieved 20 January 2012).

Steinke, Gord. *Mobsters & Rum Runners of Canada.* Edmonton: Folklore Publishing, 2003.

Chapter 19: The Kenora Bomber

"He went out with a bang." *Winnipeg Sun*, 10 May 2009. www.winnipegsun.com/news/world/2009/05/10/9411136-sun.html (retrieved 20 January 2012).

"Robber killed by own bomb." *Montreal Gazette*, 11 May 1973.

"We're tied up right now." *Montreal Gazette*, 11 May 1973.

"'Everything has gone crazy'…radio man at bank scene." *Montreal Gazette*, 11 May 1973.

"Explosion Nips Bank Robbery." *Modesto Bee*, 11 May 1973.

"Inquest finds shot at thief justified." *Ottawa Citizen*, 6 June 1973.

"Police Officers receive award." *Record News*, 5 September 1973.

Chapter 20: The Telltale Mummy

"Does mummified baby have living cousin?" *Toronto Star*, 24 September 2007. www.thestar.com/News/GTA/article/259775 (retrieved 20 January 2012).

"Who is the baby at 29 Kintyre?" *CBC News*, 17 September 2007. www.cbc.ca/news/background/kintyre/ (retrieved 20 January 2012).

Chapter 21: Early Lake Monsters

Colombo, John Robert. *Mysteries of Ontario*. Toronto: Hounslow Press, 1999.

Meurger, Michel, and Claude Gagnon. *Lake Monster Traditions: A Cross-Cultural Analysis*. London: Fortean Times, 1988.

"Tobermory's monster weekend." *Globe and Mail*, Advertising Travel Supplement, 10 July 1998.

"The Atlas of Canada: Lakes." Natural Resources Canada. atlas.nrcan.gc.ca/auth/English/learningresources/facts/lakes.html (retrieved 20 January 2012).

"The Atlas of Canada: Frequently Asked Questions About Canada." Natural Resources Canada. atlas.nrcan.gc.ca/site/English/learningresources/facts/faq.html (retrieved 20 January 2012).

"Main Duck Island History." Lake Ontario 300. www.lo300.org/event/history/main-duck-island (retrieved 20 January 2012).

Chapter 22: The Pembroke Wildman

Arment, Chad. *The Historical Bigfoot: Early Reports of Wild Men, Hairy Giants and Wandering Gorillas in North America*. Landisville, PA: Coachwhip Publications, 2006.

"Man or Gorilla? The Extraordinary Character Who is Scaring Canucks." *Newark Daily Advocate*, 1 August 1883.

Chapter 23: Old Yellowtop Sightings, a.k.a. Precambrian Shield Man

"Who's taken my fur coat? Vets baffled by bald bears with mystery condition." Daily Mail, 3 November 2009. www.dailymail.co.uk/news/article-1225042/Germanys-bald-bears-Fur-disease-afflicts-Dolores-baffles-vets.html (retrieved 22 January 2012).

The following three articles were retrieved on 22 January 2012. The dates and citations are those indicated on the OntarioSasquatch (www.ontariosasquatch. com) website, taken in turn from John Willson Green's book, *Sasquatch: The Apes Among Us*, published in 2006 by Hancock House.

Prospectors See 'Yellow Top.'" North Bay Nugget, 27 June 1923. www.ontario sasquatch.com/#/ne-article-1923-cobalt/4521050843.

"Was it 'Yellow Top.'" *North Bay Nugget*, 16 April 1946. www.ontariosasquatch. com/#/ne-article-1946-cobalt/4521050768.

"Driver Startled by Dark Form." *North Bay Nugget*, 5 August 1970. www.ontario sasquatch.com/#/ne-article-1970-cobalt/4521050657.

Chapter 24: Mid-20th-century Lake Monsters and the Birth of Igopogo

Avis, Walter S. (ed.). *A Dictionary of Canadianisms on Historical Principles.* Toronto: W.J. Gage, 1967.

Garner, Betty Sanders. *Canada's Monsters.* Hamilton: Potlatch Publications, 1976.

Kelly, Walt. *I Go Pogo.* New York: Simon and Schuster, 1952.

"Strange Tales: Indian Band Shows Fear of Monster." *Globe and Mail*, 13 August 1947.

"Lake Simcoe Has Monster, Startles Guide and Party." *Globe and Mail*, 2 August 1952.

"Kempenfelt Kelly: Is lake serpent real or just a tall tale?" Inside Ontario, *Toronto Star*, 4 April 1987.

"When Ogopogo Was Going for a Song." ShukerNature. karlshuker.blogspot.com/2010/12/when-ogopogo-was-going-for-song.html (retrieved 22 January 2012).

Chapter 25: The Beast of the Side Roads

Green, John. *The Sasquatch File.* Agassiz, BC: Cheam Publishing, 1973.

"Further Sightings of the Smithville Creature." *Beamsville Express*, 25 August 1965. www.ontariosasquatch.com/#/cen-campden-1965/4521069328 (retrieved 22 January 2012).

"Teetotal Trucker Spots 'Monster.'" *Hamilton Spectator*, 14 August 1965.

"'Monster' A Monster To Police." *Hamilton Spectator*, 17 August 1965.

Chapter 26: Monster Busters!

Bradley, Michael. *More Than a Myth: The Search for the Monster of Muskrat Lake.* Toronto: Hounslow Press, 1989.

Chapter 27: Giant Footprints in the Far North

"'Bigfoot' on the Prowl in Canadian North?" Reuters, 27 June 2001. www.ontario sasquatch.com/#/peawanuckar1/4521446551 (retrieved 22 January 2012).

"Bigfoot on Hudson Bay." *Nunatsiaq News*, 29 June 2001. www.nunatsiaqonline.ca/ archives/nunavut010630/nvt10629_22.html (retrieved 22 January 2012).

"Polar Bear." Ontario Parks. www.ontarioparks.com/English/pola.html (retrieved 22 January 2012).

Chapter 28: The Giant of Grassy Narrows

"Sasquatch Sighting has Grassy Narrows in a Buzz." *Kenora Daily Miner and News*, 26 July 2008. www.kenoradailyminerandnews.com/rticleDisplay. aspx?archive=true&e=1130596 (retrieved 23 January 2012).

"Berry-pickers report sasquatch sighting in northern Ontario." *CBC News*, 28 July 2008. www.cbc.ca/news/canada/manitoba/story/2008/07/28/ sasquatch.html (retrieved 23 January 2012).

"'Sasquatch' spotted in northern Ont." *Vancouver Sun*, 29 July 2008. www.canada.com/vancouversun/news/story.html?id=cc09c3c1-ad9c-4d34-9a5d-07dffa05271c (retrieved 23 January 2012).

"'Looked 8 feet tall.'" *Winnipeg Sun*, 28 July 2008. www.ontariosasquatch.com/ #/nw-winsun-grassy-narrows/4530330155 (retrieved 23 January 2012).

Geordie Tefler

Geordie Telfer is a writer, occasional playwright and sometime performer who lives in Toronto, Ontario. During a checkered but happily misspent youth, he was the assistant director for the Toronto Studio Players Theatre School, a freelance set carpenter and, on one occasion, the reluctant wrangler of a monkey and a ferret. Currently, he writes mainly for web and for television, having penned several documentaries that aired on Discovery Canada and Animal Planet. He fills most of his days creating content for interactive projects associated with Treehouse TV, TVOKids and for other children's broadcasters across Canada. He is also the author of three other non-fiction books.